ELEMENTS OF WAR

Volume I: Clash

Jonathan Lopez

authorHOUSE®

AuthorHouse™
1663 Liberty Drive
Bloomington, IN 47403
www.authorhouse.com
Phone: 1-800-839-8640

First published by AuthorHouse 6/16/2009

ISBN: 978-1-4389-9440-6 (sc)

*Printed in the United States of America
Bloomington, Indiana*

This book is printed on acid-free paper.

To my mom and dad
    -Thanks for not charging me rent.

About the Author

JONATHAN LOPEZ HAS ALWAYS had a unique vision of the impossible. Since he was very young he created stories in his head and retold them to his friends and family. Jonathan's family first noticed his wild imagination and creativity when he introduced them to his imaginary friend, who joined Jonathan on his wild adventures in his imaginary worlds. His imagination and creativity finally came into focus when he read his first comic book. Reading comic books and graphic novels tuned Jonathan's mind into a whole new world of struggling heroes, menacing villains, and breathtaking circumstances. Though he enjoyed reading about his favorite heroes week after week, no heroes possessed qualities he wanted to see. That is when he began thinking up, and writing about his own stories, heroes, and villains. He has received several awards in high school for his creative short stories. During his senior year in school, he started his first project, Elements Of War. After graduating high school, he completed the first installment in the trilogy, and began working on the second. As a young writer, Jonathan hopes his stories will one day be as well known as the comics he reads.

Prologue

In the beginning there was The Essence. It created the entire known universe and beyond. The origin of this force is unknown, even to those who know of its existence. The purposes of most of its creations are unknown as well. One of the few certainties in its existence is that it created all things.

One other known fact about The Essence is that the same force that created this Supreme Being also created a negative being; nothing is known of this one. The Essence was aware that its "brother" would somehow threaten its most precious creation. So The Essence hid this creation on a floating, lifeless rock. As soon as the creation touched the wasteland surface of this world, the planet flourished. The Essence then created nine powerful creatures to protect this world: The horse, the eagle, the phoenix, the rhino, the dragon, the stingray, the dove, the bat, and the mighty chimera.

These creatures were limited by their short life spans. So The Essence infused each creature with an element so that the creatures could live as long as that element existed on this world.

And so it went that generation through generation these beasts battled any and all threats to the existence of The Essence's ultimate creation. They blazed through the arctic cold of the Ice Age, and they even obliterated nearly all of existence in the savage lands of prehistory. But within the last few millennia, following the arrival of man, these warrior-beasts simply disappeared. At least, that is what we believe.

CHAPTER 1:

GENESIS

IT STARTED OFF LIKE any other day, John threw a shoe at Marc to wake him up and it was raining. Marc looked at his alarm clock to see what time it was. The clock flashed 12:00 repeatedly.

"Damn it John, did you disconnect my alarm again?" Marc asked. He couldn't hear what John was saying. All Marc could hear was thrashing music of Static X. Then he realized he still had his earmuff-sized headphones on.

"No, but I have to show you something. Get up; we have to go to the park." John said as Marc took off his headphones, got up, and went to the kitchen to check the clock on the microwave. It flashed 12:00 also.

"Jesus man, was there a blackout or something? What

time is it?" Marc asked. He went to the living room to check the clock by the front door. It wasn't ticking but it was stopped at 5:34 AM. "What the hell is wrong with our damn clocks? John what time is it?" he said frustrated. He had to be at work at noon and didn't want to be late again.

Marc was an intern at a radio station. The job wasn't what he though it would be. He thought he would meet famous musicians and bands, but he is always in the back, filing documents and getting everyone coffee and whatever else the DJs wanted. The Job was simple and rewarding, but boring. He always daydreamed. He never left Loma Linda. The only time he left was to go to collage for 3 years in New York City. It was there where he stayed with his cousin's.

"Turn on the TV and check, schmuck." John said from Marc's room.

Marc mimicked what John said in a childish way as he turned on the TV and flipped through the channels looking for the news. He stopped at a channel that was airing the news. He looked at the lower right corner of the screen. The time on the news showed it was 6:24 AM.

"Damn it John, I don't have to be at work for another five and a half hours. Why did you wake me up so damn early?" Marc complained. John walked in and threw a long sleeved shirt at Marc.

"Stop saying 'damn' and get ready. I have to show you something." John said. Marc knew something was wrong because John wasn't saying anything funny or lame. In fact, John was hardly saying anything at all.

As Marc looked back at the TV he saw that the reporter was talking about a person who had been missing for several days now. He was the son of some rich, corporate conglomerate. Marc wasn't too keen on the details but he did know that the person missing was twenty-four years old, same age as him. The reporter was talking about how there were no ransom notes or anything that would show why the person was beaten and taken from his fathers home. Marc thought nothing of it while he put the long sleeved shirt on. He was too deep in thought about why John would have woken him up so early.

"John, this better be important man." Marc said with an annoyed voice. "I mean, you keep me up till midnight because your date last night had a friend, a very weird friend, and now you wake me up early as hell. How are you even awake right now? I didn't think you would sleep last night when I saw you take your date home with you."

"Calm down. When are you ganna learn to have a little fun?" John said.

Marc was somewhat relieved to hear John talk this way. Now he knew nothing was wrong, just important.

They both exited the house and paused as Marc locked the front door. They both began walking towards John's house, which was located just down the street. They didn't enter his house, mainly because John didn't want to disturb his sister who had been working the entire night before. They simply got into John's car and went to the park. The trip was going to take a while so Marc decided to take a nap in the back seat of John's car while John drove. Marc sat with one leg up across the entire seat. He leaned his head back and fell asleep.

After arriving at Yukaipa Regional Park, John parked his '08 Cobra Mustang. He looked back at Marc through the rearview mirror as he fiddled with the silver crucifix around his neck. He then reached under the seat for something to throw at Marc.

"If you throw something at me, John, I swear I will hurt you" Marc said with his eyes' closed and his arms crossed as if he was still asleep.

"Hey, I paid the entrance fee so you better be awake." John said. Marc sighed and climbed out of the car. "Follow me, ugly." John joked as he began to climb the hill. The rain and mud didn't help. When they reached the top of the hill, John told Marc to stand off to the side and watch, just watch. Marc had no idea that what he was about to witness was the begging of something incredibly epic.

Marc stood and watched John raise one hand into the air. He had no idea what John was doing. Marc wasn't sure what he was looking at until he heard thunder. Both of them looked up into the sky. The thundering sound in the sky got closer. Marc got nervous and a little scared as he saw lightning flicker in the clouds. Then, in an instant, a massive bolt of lightning struck John's hand. Marc fell back onto the floor. He was wide-awake now. His heart was pounding like a jackhammer now. John, on the other hand, wasn't scared. Oh no, John was laughing.

"You want to see another one?" he asked with a smile on his face. Two more slammed into his hand, one after the other. Loud booms followed each one. At this point, even Marc was laughing from the ground, he hadn't stood back up after his fall. He thought he was losing his mind. Then something unexpected happened.

A bolt that came down at an odd angle curved and missed John's hand and hit the ground, inches from Marc's feet. The voltage coursed through his body and paralyzed him in pain. Every muscle in his body tightened. He couldn't move, he couldn't react, and then he realized he couldn't breath. His lungs and heart stopped moving. John ran to him and put his ear to Marc's chest. He didn't hear a heart beat. *Oh Jesus Christ* John thought to himself. He was scared and panicking. He thought he was going to have a heart attack. Then he had a brilliant idea.

Marc, Please God, let this work; John continued to think to himself. He closed both his fist and rubbed his knuckles together. After rubbing them for a few seconds, his knuckles began to hum. Then he pressed both knuckles against Marc's chest. His body jumped as John's knuckles met his chest. John did this three more times before Marc started breathing again. Marc sat up and looked at John.

"There are so many reasons why that shouldn't have worked" John joked to Marc.

"Did you just defibrillate me?" Marc asked as he stood up.

"Well I can tell you the truth or we can just ignore this whole moment in our lives." John said as he helped Marc up.

"I think I'm going to ignore it Johnny boy, you could do whatever you..." Marc suddenly stopped talking as his eyes' began to turn from a light brown to neon blue. John took a step back. Marc clutched his stomach and began to groan, not in pain but in a way that can only be described as straining. He was trying to hold something in but he didn't know what. Then, finally, he let it go. Massive waves of electricity blasted from his body. The bolts dug into and scorched everything they hit. Luckily they were on a hill. No one else was on the hill so no one else was hit or saw it happen. John was hit but it didn't seem to hurt him. Marc dropped to his knees and tried to pull it all back in.

"I can't stop it!" He yelled at John. John knew how to stop this. He started to walk towards Marc; forcing his way through each wave of electricity that blasted it's way out of Marc. Every wave came out with loud boom. Finally he got to Marc and grabbed him and yelling.

"Listen to me Marc, you gatta focus man. Try to calm down and slow your heart rate. Right now that's what is throwing you into overdrive. Just focus and calm down. Breath!" Marc closed his eyes and took in a few deep breaths. Then the blasts began to weaken and fade. Then, after a short while, it just stopped.

The car ride home was as silent as the ride to the park, only now it was acquired. John finally broke the silence.

"It happened to me about two weeks ago." John started. "I was leaving the theater and the light post I was under, like, went into overdrive and popped. Then my heart started to beat faster and faster. After about four seconds of that, the same kind of sparks flew out of me. Lucky for me, no one was there. I was the only one there cause I was leaving last."

"Well that's super, John. Why didn't you tell me this before, man?" Marc asked. He felt betrayed. He didn't think John would hide such a big secret from him. John took a moment to answer.

"Well I was scared. I thought I was losing my mind at first. Then I started to experiment with it a little and now I can do some neat stuff with it. So I decided to show you now." Mark looked at John like he said something unbelievably dense.

When they got to Marc's house, John had told Marc to call in sick to work. Of course, Marc would comply. As soon as Marc walked in, he grabbed the phone and called the station. When his supervisor's assistant answered, he asked to speak to his supervisor.

"Hey, Carl, I don't think I can make it to work today." Said Marc.

"Oh that's ok Marc. Is there something wrong, are you ok?"

"I just got this headache and I've been dizzy and I feel like I'm going to pass out." The irony in Marc saying this is that he was actually starting to feel like that.

"Well that's ok. Just take it easy. Bye" his supervisor hung up. Marc began to walk to the living room to tell John that he really wasn't feeling well. John turned from the TV to Marc. He saw Marc was walking like he had been hit on the head with a hammer.

"Marc, are you ok?" John asked, but it was to late; Marc had collapsed and gone unconscious.

CHAPTER 2:

THE INTRODUCTION

MARC OPENED HIS EYES and saw he was in a desert. He got up off the floor and looked around. The dry, rocky ground was a sapphire color, which of course is odd. He looked up at the sky and saw thick, intimidating storm clouds. He could hear the faint roar of thunder in the distance. There was a cold wind that sent chills down his spine. He looked out into the distance, but the desert seemed to go on forever.

Then he heard a voice from behind him say, "Do not be alarmed Chimera. This is the Nexus."

Marc turned to face whoever was talking to him. What he saw was a man that looked oddly like him. Only instead of being 6'1" he was 7'7" and had long brown hair instead of short hair. He looked a bit more muscular than Marc.

"Who are you?" Marc asked. The man standing in front of him began to walk around Marc.

"I am . . . you can call me The First." Marc caught the man's hesitance.

"The First? What's your real name? And what was that thing you called me just now?" Marc was not sparing any time in asking questions.

"I cannot tell you my real name, I'm sorry I just can't. But, as for what I called you, the Chimera Sentinel." The man continued to circle Marc as he spoke. Marc had more questions.

"What is a Chimera Sentinel? And why can't you tell me your name?" Marc's main concern was trying to figure out the man's name.

"The Chimera Sentinel is the leader of the Terra Sentinels. They are the soldiers of the Earth. Your purpose in life is to protect the earth and all those who dwell within it." The man had a smile on his face as he looked at the expression on Marc's face. Marc still didn't understand what 'The First' was telling him. Last night he was just a normal guy and now he is supposed to understand that he is the leader of some group of soldiers that protect the entire world.

"Don't worry, I was flipping out too, man. But my Guide helped me through it pretty well." The image of the man changed from intimidating to just plain odd after that last statement. Marc was now confused. How is he supposed to believe a man that spoke like that? "If you must know, I'm fifty-one. Or at least I'm supposed to be. I'm stuck in this twenty-seven year olds body for the rest of 'your' life."

Marc thought it was his turn to talk, "Wait, what do

you mean? Your not going to kill me, are you?"

"Oh God, no, I'm only here till you die, at which time, you will become the next Chimera Sentinel's Guide. I'm your Guide. I'm here to help you with whatever you need. So, what do you need?" Marc looked around, then only one question came to mind, "Well where are we exactly? This place looks like the damn desert."

The 'First' looked around and looked at the ground beneath him. Then, in an instant, the area changed from an odd desert to a sunny, beautiful beach. Marc jumped as he heard the sound of waves crash against a rock formation in the water.

"How did you do that? Where are we now?" Marc asked looking around franticly.

The First answered with a condescending voice, "Well we're in your head so things change when you or I think about it. Come on man, keep up." Marc was no longer nervous. In fact, he had a smile on his face. He felt like The First was no threat to him. He sat down in the sand; The First sat down next to him. Marc had a few more questions.

"So what are the Sentinels really?" The First looked at him and then to the water. After a few seconds, nine people walked out of the water and stood before them.

"Don't worry, they're not real. They are just images I'm making. These are this generation's Sentinels. Look at all eight of them." Marc looked puzzled for a few moments.

"There are nine here. Not eight." Marc said.

"Holy crap, your right!" The first stood up and walked around, inspecting all nine people. "Oh well there are twins here." He said pointing out two girls. The twins and everyone else looked about the same age. Marc got up and inspected everyone as well. He noticed a familiar man in the line-up.

The man was a bit shorter than him. He had short dark brown hair that was wavy. The clothes are what especially gave away his identity. A shirt that said 'Will work for head' and had a picture of a headless stick figure. And pants that were at least two sizes too big.

"What is John doing here?" he asked The First. The First turned to see whom he was talking about.

"Oh, the Luther kid. Yeah, he's a Sentinel." Marc wasn't surprised to find that out after what happened on the hill earlier that day.

"So what makes us so special? How are we supposed to protect the earth?" Marc asked as he looked through the roster of strangers.

"Well Marc, you use the weapons that the earth provides. The elements. John, for example, is the Thunder-horse Sentinel."

"Thunder-horse?" Marc said, puzzled.

"Yes, the sentinels are defined by an animal and element. John is the Thunder-horse and you are the Omni-Chimera." Marc sat down.

"So, um, The First, what element is omni?" The First sat down next to Marc again.

"Well Marc, all of them. You are to control all nine elements." Marc was confused for a moment. He simply shook his mind of a thought that was confusing him.

He looked up at The First, "Can you tell me what these elements are?"

"Sure thing. Well there is Omni-Chimera, Thunder-Horse, Flame-Phoenix, Spectral-Dove, Sonic-Bat, Gale-Eagle, Tidal-Stingray, Rock-Rhino, and Bio-Dragon."

"Am I supposed to meet these people eventually?" Marc asked as he looked at a tall woman who was standing at the end of the line-up. He thought she was beautiful. She was 6'3"; she had long, light brown hair. Her skin was tan and she had a face that looked like it could stop traffic.

"Are you asking because you want to meet them all or because you think that the Bio-Dragon is cute?" Marc turned to look at The First. He tried to speak but no words would come out, only stutters. He felt embarrassed.

"It's ok, you know. The Bios usually do that to people. They are always gorgeous girls. But to answer your question, yes. You have to meet everyone to gain his or her element. Don't worry. I know where each one is. I'll tell you, in just a second, where the closest one is" The First's eyes began to glow a bright green as he stared off into space.

"Why are we getting these powers now?" Marc asked as he watches The First.

"Your abilities only activate when there is an imminent threat approaching." The First said.

"I see." Marc said as he thought about what he just heard.

"The closest one, besides your friend, is in Mexico. In the state of Chihuahua. Her name is Ignacia Castillo. She is Fire-Phoenix." The First went back to normal. "Well hey, I have to let you wake up now. Take care of yourself kiddo. Just think about me and I'll show up again. Also, every time you gain an element, prepare to lose control for a few seconds. So go somewhere secluded when you do." Marc nodded and stood up. The First stood up and extended his hand to Marc. Marc looked at it and shook it with his.

"Oh, and how did you know my name anyway?" Marc asked as they shook hands.

The First merely laughed, "There isn't a thing I don't know about you, Marcus Salazar Jr." Marc shuttered at the sound of his whole name, his father's name.

At that moment, he woke up. He looked around and saw he was in his room. He could hear the TV in the living room.

"John, is that you?" He shouted. John ran into the room.

"Damn, your finally awake." Marc sat up in bed; he rubbed his eyes.

"How long was I out for, Johnny?" John looked at his watch and answered,

"Going on three days now. Marc, you had me worried. The doctor said you were just sleeping though, so he said to just let you sleep. What happened?" Marc looked at his hands.

"John, I have to tell you something." Marc said as he moved to the edge of the bed.

"Jesus, your not coming out to me, are you?" joked John.

"No, just listen. And after I need you to take me to my mom's house." John looked at Marc with serious eyes, something that doesn't happen very often.

"Sure thing." He said as Marc stood up and walked towards the kitchen. John sat at the table as Marc turned on the coffee maker. "So what is it?" John asked. Marc sat down next to him.

"Well, I'm not too sure how to say this, but . . ."

CHAPTER 3:

FORGOTTEN HISTORY

"WELL, MARC, I HAVE to tell you, this is a little unbelievable. But who am I to argue, I hit you with lightning a few days ago and you, sort of, exploded." John said as he took the car around the corner.

"I know, it sounds like something from a comic book or that damn Wizard Magazine, but it's true." Said Marc.

"Well we're here." John said as they pulled up to Marc's mother's house. As Marc stepped out of the car, John said, "Hey I'm going to the liquor store really quick, to get something to drink. That coffee gave me cotton-mouth."

Marc nodded his head and said, "Sure thing man. I won't be here long." John drove away. Marc began walking up the driveway to his mother's home. He was thinking about his childhood along the way. With every step, another memory. His mother was always there for him. She was the only one that was there. His father left his mother when she was still pregnant with Marc. He was never told why but he despised his father for this.

Marc stood in front of his mother's doorstep. He knocked and said, "Mom, are you home? It's Marc." His mother opened the door.

"Hi baby, what are you doing here?" She hugged him and let him in. He entered and saw Chuck, Marc's stepfather, sitting in a recliner.

"Hey Marc. What happened? Are you ok? How long have you been up?" Chuck asked as he stood up to give Marc a hug.

"Hey dad," said Marc as he hugged Chuck.

Marc loved Chuck like it was his real father. Chuck had married Marina Salazar when Marc was Seven years old. He helped shape Marc into the man he was today. Chuck was the closest thing Marc had to a father. He even took John in when his father kicked him out of his house when they were fifteen. That is why Marc calls him 'dad'.

"I'm just here to talk to my mom about something. How are you doing pop?" asked Marc as he sat down on the couch next to the recliner. Chuck sat down on the recliner and looked at Marc.

"What do you need to talk to your mom about?" Marc paused for a moment to think for an answer. After a few seconds he finally answered.

"Oh, just some medical things." Chuck nodded. "Mom, do you think we can talk in private? It's kind of embarrassing." Marc asked his mother.

"Hey, you know what, just talk in the kitchen. I was

going to the store right now anyway." Said Chuck as he stood back up.

As Marc and his mother sat at the table, Chuck grabbed his car keys and headed out the door.

"Mom, this isn't a medical question. I'm just here to ask for a few hundred bucks to get me and John to Mexico for a while." Said Marc, the instant the door closed. He said almost in a whisper. His mother looked shocked and scared.

"Marcus, what's wrong? Are you and John in some sort of trouble?" She asked franticly.

"No mom, it's nothing like that. Calm down. I just need to go meet some people. I won't be gone long." Marc answered with a reassuring voice. She then thought for a moment and looked into Marc's eyes.

"Does this have anything to do with you being asleep for three days?" She asked. It didn't look like she needed an answer.

"Yeah, it sort of does." Marc answered.

She stood up and walked to a window. She stared out into the world and sighed depressingly.

"Mom, what's wrong? Are you ok?" Marc asked.

"Oh, I'm fine, I was just thinking of your father." Marc got up angrily.

"Damn it mom! What is wrong with you? The guy left you a month before I was born and you always think of him! Why now? Is it because you think I won't come back? Damn it mom, I'm not like that bastard." Marc shouted with rage.

"Don't you dare talk about your father that way! He was a good man." Marc's anger grew.

"A 'good man'? You said he left you without even saying a word! If he is such a good man then where the hell is he? You know what, never mind. I'll just get to Mexico some other way!" Marc shouted as he walked towards the front door.

Marc slammed the door behind him as he left. He began to walk to the corner of the Redlands blvd. and Mountain View. As he got there, John pulled up.

"What happened man? You look pissed." John stated as he slowed the car to a stop. Marc opened the passenger side door and got in.

"I'm ok man. Let's just go to my house." Marc said as he buckled his seatbelt with force. His facial expression wasn't convincing. He looked angry. His eyes were full of rage.

John nodded and simply said, "Uh-huh. Well are we still going to Mexico?" Marc sat and though for a moment, looking down at his feet. He began to smile and slowly looked up at John.

"Only if you're down to drive." He said trying not to laugh at what he just said. John thought for a moment.

"Hell yeah!" John swiftly shifted the car into gear. The tires screeched as the car sped off towards Marc's house.

"I'll stop by your house when I'm done packing." John said to Marc as he parked his car in front of his house. Marc nodded and climbed out of the car. John turned the alarm of his car on as he walked into his house. When he walked into his house he heard his niece.

"Uncle, hi." She said as she ran up to hug him. His sister was washing dishes.

"Hey Camille, I have to tell you something, so we have to talk later." He said as he walked to his room.

She simply said "Yup."

His sister was a single mother. Her husband had left her and their daughter, Sabrina, two years ago. After a few months, John had convinced her to buy a house near his and Marcs. To help pay for it, he moved out of Marc's house and moved in with her. After all, Marc didn't need help paying rent for his house, on a count that his mother is a doctor and his stepfather is a lawyer. John's sister was a short woman. She was three years older than John, making her twenty-eight. She looked a lot younger though, like nineteen. She was the only real family, besides Marc, that he had.

As Camille walked into John's room, she saw he was packing his things. She looked at a complete loss for a moment.

Finally she asked, "So what's up? What did you need to talk to me about?" John looked up from stuffing a shirt into his duffle bag.

"Oh hey, I'm going to look for some girl in Mexico for a few days with Marc." He said plainly, as if it were no big deal.

"Um, ok. Let me ask again. What are you doing?" She said. She looked like she was getting annoyed. John wasn't a desirable roommate. He stayed up till all hours of the night, he cursed a lot, and most of his friends were shady characters. So you could understand why Camille would get annoyed easily with John.

"Well, Marc has to meet with a friend of his in Mexico and I'm going to drive him there. Is that ok 'mother'?" he asked a tad condescendingly. She scoffed.

"How do you plan on paying for this 'little' trip of yours? You plan on whoring yourself out to some people or something?" she asked. John stopped packing for a moment and thought about an answer.

"The thought had crossed my mind, yes. But you know Marc and me, we have are ways of getting around. Remember that time we got lost at that fair? We were nine and me and Marc still beat you home." John said with a smile on his face.

"Yeah John, but you didn't need money for that. Why do you need to go anyway? If it's him that needs to meet this person then let him go by himself. I don't see why you would have to go." Camille argued. "What about Sabrina? Did you think of her? What am I supposed to tell her? That her Uncle John had to go away for a while because he's an idiot."

"No, just tell her I had to go on a trip for a while and that I'll bring her back a sombrero. She won't even miss me." John said. Camille stared into John's eyes. She new there was no changing his mind once he made his decision.

"Fine, just let me give you a few bucks for the trip." Camille said as she walked to her room. John smiled and started packing again. Camille walked back in, holding three, hundred-dollar bills.

"Thanks sis, I appreciate it." He said as he took the money and gave her a big bear-like hug.

"Yeah, just bring me back a sombrero too you little bastard." She said jokingly.

When John got back to his car, it was 9:47 PM. He turned his car on and made a U-turn to Marc's house, and parked right in front of it. When he entered Marc's house he went directly to Marc's room. That's where John saw him in some sort of trance. He was still packing his bag. He looked as if he was frozen in time. John just stood there without knowing what to do. Then Marc just started moving again. The sudden thrust into motion that Marc made, startled John.

"Whoa man. Is this going to happen a lot?" he asked Marc nervously.

"Relax John, this guy was just telling me what city to look in."

"Well where?" John asked.

"Delicias, Chihuahua." Marc said. John leaned against the doorway and thought for a moment.

"Dude, they don't eat dog, do they?" he asked. Marc looked up at him like he was crazy.

"It's not even pronounced the same as delicious, you moron." Marc said, trying not to laugh.

John and Marc walked outside and began walking to the car. Just before they got to the car, a blue Ford Explorer pulled up. It was Marc's mother. She stepped out of the passenger side; Chuck was driving. She walked towards them. John looked shy, as he always did around her.

"Hello John, maybe you should go and put Marc's bags in your car." She said to John as if he were a child.

"Yes Mrs. Salazar, I mean Mrs. House." John said awkwardly. John had always called her Mrs. Salazar except in front of Marc. He never knew why. John took Marc's backpack and duffle bag and walked to his car.

Marc spoke first.

"I'm sorry about earlier mom. I didn't mean to go off on you like that. I mean," just as he was speaking, his mother interrupted.

"Listen Marc, I understand that you 'believe' you have to go. So I'm here to give you this." She gave him a check she had been holding. Marc looked at it and it was a check for twelve hundred dollars.

"If you need any more, just call." She said. Marc gave

her a hug; she hugged him back. When he let go he looked down.

"Mom, I may have to go to other places before I come back home." He said with regret in his voice.

She simply responded, "I know."

She hugged him one more time and walked away. As she walked by John, who was leaning on the hood of his car, she hugged him and said, "Take care of my son. He's all you got."

John hugged her back and said, "Yes ma'am. Always."

As Chuck and Marc's mom drove away, John and Marc got into the Mustang. They were both quiet for a moment.

Then John said, "Man, your mom is hot." Marc punched him on the shoulder and laughed.

"Lets go, jackass." Marc said. John threw the car into gear and began driving away.

Chapter 4:

Ignition

John walked up the street with a brown paper bag in hand. He kept looking at a '68 302 Boss Mustang that just parked across the street. He knew that the owner of the car was the particular girl that he and Marc had been looking for. He just didn't expect her to be so beautiful. As the door opened, a young girl stepped out of the driver-side door. John pretended to not be looking at her as she looked around. He almost tripped over an elevated sidewalk as he crossed the street. *Smooth moron,* he thought to himself.

The girl was short, her hair was to her solders and a dark brown, and her face was the prettiest face that John had ever seen. The strangest thing is that she never wore skirts, dresses, or anything else a normal girl would ware, and she always had an angry look on her eyes. She always carried a duffle bag to where ever it is she went, and came home tired and sweaty. John didn't understand why.

John walked a few more blocks towards the motel that he and Marc were staying at. When he walked in, he saw Marc sitting up in his bed and making sparks fly from one hand to the other. John threw the bag at him.

"Here, eat your burrito and lets go talk to her. I'm tired of waiting. She just got home and she is ALONE!" he said a bit angry. They had been waiting for three days but were lagging because they didn't know what to say that didn't sound crazy.

"What do you want to tell her? That we are soldiers from the earth sent to 'copy' her fire powers, and that the fate of the world depends on it?" Marc said sarcastically. John sat down.

"Yeah, sounds good to me." John said earnestly. Marc rolled his eyes. "Look, if she knows that she has these powers then she will believe us. Right?" John pointed out. Marc stopped playing with his electric hands.

"I think you just said something smart." He said to John.

After Marc 'inhaled' his burrito, they set out to talk to her. They were both nervous as they approached her house. When they reached her door, John looked at Marc and nodded his head at the door. Marc slapped John on the back of the head and knocked on the door. The young woman answered and looked at both of them.

"Buenos tardes." She said. Just as Marc was about to speak, John through his hand over Marcs mouth.

"Me lamo John," John started in horrible Spanish. "El is my amigo," she interrupted him before he could butcher more of the language.

"I speak English, zángano." She said with a thick accent.

"What does that mean?" John asked, putting down the hand that kept Marc from speaking.

"Jackass. God is he always this dense?" she asked. Marc nodded.

"Oh, by the way, I talked to her while you were out." Marc said with a smile on his face

"So are you almost packed?" Marc asked from Ignacia's couch. She was in her room packing all her things. When she heard they were going to make a world tour, she just had to go along.

"Yeah, I'm almost done. So where are we going from here?" she shouted. Marc closed his eyes and thought of The First. Then everything turned black for a moment.

He was sitting on the couch in the desert. When he turned to look around he saw The First sitting next to him.

"Hey," said the first somewhat cheerfully. "What do you need Marc?" It was a bit intimidating to sit next to such a mountain of a man.

"Where do we go from here?" The First looked out into space again, his eyes turning a bright green.

Finally, after a while, The First said, "Well there are two in El Salvador and one in Brazil. So you can pick those three off right now. The two in El Salvador are the twins so it's just one element." Marc looked at The First and nodded.

"Well, I should get going. I'll see you in a little bit." Said Marc and shook The First's hand again.

The First laughed and said, "Any time buddy, just remember, take cover when you take each one." He warned.

Marc responded, "Got it."

Marc opened his eyes. He was still on the couch and Ignacia was still packing. In fact, only three seconds had passed. He looked around the living room. John was looking at family pictures and little religious ornaments that plagued the shelves around the TV set and bookshelves.

"Having fun, numb-nuts?" Marc asked John. He almost dropped a statue of Jesus he was currently inspecting.

"Hey," John started nervously, "did you even get her abilities yet?" he asked.

"Yeah, we went to this field where she experimented with her powers and I kinda exploded a second crater in that area." Marc answered. Ignacia walked in.

"I'm done." She exclaimed. John looked her up and down. She was wearing denim shorts and a tight blue shirt. John just looked up at Marc and smiled. Marc knew what John was thinking, which was a bad thing. Marc knew if anything happened between them two something would go wrong, especially if John was associated. Marc just sighed.

"So let's get going then people." John said. As they walked outside, John noticed Ignacia was walking away from his car. She caught his look of confusion.

"I'm going to fallow you in my car." She said. John looked at her classic, beautiful car. In an instant, John threw his keys at Marc, who had just barley caught them, and ran to her.

"You have to let me drive." John pleaded. She stared at him for a moment.

"If I say no, will you leave me alone?" she asked innocently.

"No." John responded rather quickly.,

"Just let him drive. He won't leave you alone till you do." Marc yelled from John's car, which was across the street. She stared at John and thought for a moment.

"Fine, but I'm riding with you, because this car is my baby." She said.

Jesus Christ, another one, Marc thought. John cheered and took the keys from her hands.

It was weird for John to be fallowing his own car. He also noticed that the car he was driving had more power than his. This hurt him a bit, he had done almost everything he could think of to his car but it was still weaker than some. He turned to look at Ignacia and saw she was looking bored already.

"So who were you living with anyway? I saw that you had pictures of a lot of people in your living room." He said to break the silence.

"I was living with my grandma and my cousins. They won't care if I leave though. They have been suggesting I leave for a while." She said with a depressed voice.

"Why is that?" John asked.

"Well they are my stepmother's relatives, not mine. They have been trying to make me leave because they don't like me." She told John.

"What happened to your parents and your stepmother?" He asked. She looked a bit more relaxed for some reason.

"My mother died giving birth to me and my father died with my stepmother in a car accident two years ago." She said. John looked at the road ahead but had what Ignacia just said in mind.

He looked at her and said, "Your lucky, my parents were assholes. My dad beat the crap out of me when I did something 'not his way'. And my mom drank vodka like it was water. Half the time she was passed out drunk when my dad beat my sister and me. So sorry if you story isn't that sad to me, Ignacia." She didn't say anything for a while. The silence was awkward; John felt he said something wrong.

Finally she said, "It's Nacha." John looked at her, confused. She responded to his look of bewilderment, "You can call me Nacha instead of Ignacia. I don't really like my whole name."

John nodded, "Oh, right."

"So what do you do, John?" She asked. "What is your element?"

John slowed down the car near a stop sign. The sign was on the passenger side of the car. He raised his hand so that it was going across Nacha's face and pointed out the window at the sign. After a few seconds, a small jolt of electricity came out and hit sign. The sign bent and the tube holding it up seemed to melt a bit.

"What do you do Nacha?" John asked as he started to drive again.

She smiled and put one hand on his lap. John was a bit startled by this movement, but he kept on driving.

After a while she asked, "Do you feel that heat?" John began to smile, but it was quickly wiped off his face when he smelled smoke. He looked down and saw that Nacha's hand had ignited and his pants were burning.

"Oh what the hell!" John yelled as he began to pat out the fire. The flame was small so it went out almost immediately. "You could have just told me. What the hell?" John continued with an angry look on his face. Ignacia was laughing. John thought her laugh was adorable, and it was. It made him smile and forget that his jeans had a hole, the size of the palm of Ignacia's hand, burned over his knee.

CHAPTER 5:

INSOMNIA

ALL THREE WERE SITTING in the motel room. Marc had his eyes closed in a meditative state. He was sitting on one of the beds with his feet and his back against the wall with his arms crossed. John was sitting on the floor at the foot of the bed and with his back against the bed; he was watching TV. Ignacia was sitting on a chair in the corner of the room; she was staring at Marc with curiosity.

"Is he going to be ok?" she asked. John turned his head and looked at her then at Marc.

"Oh, he'll be fine. Don't worry. He's probably just trying to figure out where we're going next." Ignacia looked confused for a moment.

Then she asked, "How does he determine where to go and what we look like?" John got up and sat on the bed next to Marc's.

"Well he goes to this weird little world in his head, where a guy who had this job before him tells him what you look like and where you are." John explained.

"That sounds crazy." Ignacia said.

"This coming from a girl that can heat up her lunch by touching it." John said while remembering an incident that happened earlier that day. Ignacia looked at him and nodded. She got up and walked over to the bed that John was laying on and laid down.

"Whoa, what are you doing?" John asked, as she got comfortable.

"Well I'm getting ready for bed. Is that a problem?" She said as she kicked off her shoes. John turned his body to face her.

"Well, you got the bed last night and now it's my turn." He said.

"But I'm a girl and I always get the bed." She laughed. John thought for a moment.

Finally he said, "I have a compromise."

"Well what is it?" Ignacia asked.

"Since this is somewhat of a big bed, why don't just lay head-to-toe?" he answered. He laid down with his shoulders by her feet and his feet by her head.

"Oh God, just don't take off your shoes." She joked.

"So how long have you two been on the road?" she asked. John put his hands behind his head.

"Well plus the two days we've been riding with you, and your amazing car, about eight days." he answered.

"Now let me ask you a question. Ever since your 'abilities' came up, have you ever gone to bed tired?" he said. Ignacia sat up.

"Well no actually. I only go to sleep at night because I thought I had to. I actually don't think I have to sleep any more." She said. "Also," she continued, "I've been boxing for like six years but I've never had muscles like these before." She lifted her shirt up past her abdomen. John looked, in amazement, at her six-pack.

"Wow that is . . . did you say boxing?" he said. She put her shirt down.

"Well where did you think I went that made me so sweaty?" she asked. John thought for moment.

" I don't know I just thought you went to your boyfriend's house." John said. Ignacia laughed at his response.

"Yeah right, me have a boyfriend. Please, like I would waste my time with some boy." John sat up.

"Why not? Are you a . . ." he stopped before continuing.

"No I'm not, but what kind of guy would want to go out with a girl who could beat him up?" she said. John laid back down.

"Well, some guys may think you're kind of cute." He started blushing. "So anyway," John said after a long pause, "have you noticed that you might be able to run a little faster, and go a little further? Also hit a little harder and lift a little more?" he asked. She laid back as well.

"Well every day actually. I knew it wasn't normal for me to improve so much one day after an other." She said.

"Maybe we're being made into these 'super soldiers' for some kind of war?" John said. He noticed Ignacia shuttered at the idea of a major battle that they would have to one-day fight. He understood her fear; even he was scared of the idea.

Marc's body jumped as he woke up. John and Ignacia sat up, John turned to hang his feet off the bed and to face Marc.

"Well guys," Marc said, "it looks like we're not going to El Salvador. The spectral sentinel is just off the map. So we're just going straight towards Brazil." John stood up and stretched.

"Well now is just as good as time as any to get going." John said.

"Well if you guys want to sleep first to rest up it's fine." Marc said.

John and Ignacia looked at each other and at the same time they said, "We aren't tired."

CHAPTER 6:

JAKE EVENS

As JOHN AND IGNACIA continued talking in her classic car, John noticed Marc started to slow down his car. In response, John also started to slow down. Finally, John and Ignacia saw that Marc was picking up a rather shady looking character. The man looked like a drifter, someone who had been on the road for a while. He only had one bag, a backpack, and it looked full to maximum capacity. He was wearing a long green coat and a beat-up pair of Jeans that were rather baggy. John immediately drove the car and stopped it in front of the car Marc was in then got out.

"What the hell are you doing man?" John asked as he walked towards the blue mustang. Marc got out and stood by the open door. "Man, you can't just pick up hitch-hikers.

What are you thinking?" John asked as he reached Marc.

"Look John, calm down. I know this guy ok. It's one of Jeff's friends." Marc answered. John looked through the windshield to look at the man's face.

"Holy shit, it's Jake. What's up, man?" John exclaimed when the man's face became familiar.

John handed Ignacia her keys.

"Marc, let me ride with Jake. We have a lot to catch up on." John requested. Ignacia seemed a bit put down when she heard this. Marc looked at John and then at Jake. Jake shrugged.

"Fine." He said finally. John nabbed the keys from Marc's hand and jumped into his car. As Marc walked to Ignacia's, the blue mustang whizzed by quickly.

"Wow, he didn't waste time, did he?" Ignacia said a bit depressed.

"Don't worry, he's an idiot."Marc said as he caught her distress. Ignacia got in the driver side, and once Marc got in the passenger side, they drove off behind John.

* * *

"Damn man, I haven't seen you since graduation. How have you been?" John said with excitement in his voice.

"Well I'm sure you heard from Jeff that I washed out of boot camp." Jake said. John nodded.

"Yeah, that's like the last I heard of you until now. How did you end up her in Brazil?" John said. Jake thought for a moment.

"Well, I'm here looking for a few other friends of mine. I'm kind of requiting for the marines now."Jake said. John still had a few more questions.

"Why were you walking though? Don't they give you a car or something?" Jake leaned back in his seat.

"Yeah, but my damn Hummer broke down up the road." Jake pointed as they approached a green Hummer that was parked on the side of the road.

Jake didn't seem like the type of person to be associated with the marines. He looked like the type of guy you copy off of you during a test. Jake and Jeff were roommates back in collage. Jeff was a friend of John's since high school. That is how John and Marc met Jake. All three of them had to watch out for Jake, he was constantly being picked on and bullied, even in collage. Except the last semester of their senior year, when Jake threw a haymaker punch at one of the guys that was bullying him around. Jake knocked the guy out with that punch but the guy's friends were there and they advanced on him. Lucky for Jake, John and Jeff were there.

John found it hard to believe that the marines kept Jake, even as a recruiter. He just didn't seem the type.

"Well why are you here." Jake asked. John didn't really know what to say.

"Marc is here to visit some friend of his. I thought I should come down with him and keep him company." John said. Jake nodded.

"What about the girl? Who is she?" Jake asked.

"Oh, she's one of my friends who decided to come along for the hell of it." John said. "So what's in the bag man?" John asked as he looked at the heavy looking backpack.

"Oh just some gear and supplies." Jake said nervously for some reason.

"Ok. Do you have to carry all that crap around with you everywhere?" John asked.

"Well yeah. It's all standard issue equipment. I can't afford to lose any of it." Jake said as they entered the next town.

"Hey, can you drop me off at that warehouse over there?" Jake said pointing at a big warehouse down the street.

"Sure thing Evens. Hey keep in touch man. Do you have a cell?" John asked as he approached the warehouse.

"Yeah, let me get your number." Jake said as he pulled out his cell phone.

"Where do you think they are going?" Ignacia asked as John's car parked in front of the warehouse. Marc read the sign by the door. It read 'Chimer-Tech'. Marc knew he heard that name before. Of course, it was the name of the company that Abraham Truman owned. He was the father of the missing, twenty-four year-old guy that was on the news. Marc and Ignacia saw Jake get out of the car and walk into the building. What business does Jake have with a major medical company like Chimer-Tech?

"Hey, aren't you a chimera?" Ignacia asked.

"Yeah, so?" Marc said. "Well the first half of the company's name is Chimer. Isn't that weird?" she asked. Marc thought this was a bit odd. John shut the car down.

"John is going to want to switch me cars now." Marc said with a smile on his face. Ignacia's face lit up when she heard that. John got out and walked towards the red mustang. Marc got out of the car and took the keys from John as he walked past him. John got into the passenger seat and both cars drove away.

Meanwhile, back at the warehouse, Jake used a rather thick keycard to open the front door. When he entered, he was surrounded by machinery that was attaching mechanical limbs to dead, motionless bodies. All the bodies had dog tags on them. They were all soldiers that were either missing in action or killed in combat. Jake took off his coat; half his upper body was replaced with machinery. Both arms to his wrists, both shoulders, part of his neck, his entire back, and finally, his legs; were all mechanical. A man walked towards him from the back of the warehouse.

"Did you find them?" the man asked.

"Yes sir. I actually know them personally. They gave me enough information we need to track them." Jake replied.

"Fallow me," the man said, "I have something for you." Jake fallowed the man to the back of the warehouse. "Sit down." The man said as he pointed at a metallic chair. Jake sat down. A giant machine lowered itself over Jakes body, which was being restrained by the chair. Jake's entire body disappeared under the machine as it turned on. All that was audible was an electrical whirring like a drill, then the tearing of flesh with Jake's screams of pain, then clanking of metal with more drilling. Flashes of light were seen coming out from under the machine.

When the machine finally lifted, Jake was no longer a man. His entire body was now entirely incased in steel, including his head, which was covered by a helmet and a mask. The mask was in the shape of an eagles head. "Welcome to the A.E.S militia . . . Apollo." The man said.

CHAPTER 7:

TREE HUGGERS

IGNACIA WAS SUNBATHING ON the hood of her car while John lay in the back seat of his car with both doors open. Marc was in Ignacia's car playing with the radio.

"So how much longer do we have to sit here and wait?" asked John as he sat up. Marc got out of his car and looked around.

"Well the Brazilian soccer team is set to meet members of the Peace Corps for some publicity or something. The team is here so now we're just waiting for the members from the Peace Corps. She is with them." Marc said. John got out of his car and looked around the parking lot of the stadium.

"So it's another 'she' huh?" John asked. He had a smile on his face.

Ignacia sighed. John turned to look at her. She was wearing a bikini top and denim shorts. John just simply stared at her on the hood of her car. Marc stared at John and smiled. He knew John had a crush on Ignacia and he also knew Ignacia had some feelings for John. It was as noticeable as the blazing sun in the sky. Marc finally decided to break the silence.

"You're going to want to get down soon. You'll get one hell of a sun burn." Marc said. John snapped out of his hypnosis.

"What? No she doesn't. She's the Fire Sentinel damn it. She won't get burned." John said. Ignacia smiled with relief at hearing this. *Oh yeah, he likes me*, she thought to herself.

"If anything, she should be getting stronger." John continued. Marc looked up at him in confusion.

"How do you figure?" Ignacia asked. John looked back up at her.

"Well, have you ever read a comic book?" John said. Marc laughed at John's theory. Then John turned and saw a tour bus.

"Is that our mark . . . Marc?" John asked awkwardly. Marc turned to look at the bus. His eyes turned from light brown to dark green.

"Yup. That's her." Marc replied.

Ignacia jumped off the hood of her car and jumped into the back seat. She began changing. John and Marc quickly looked away.

"So you know what to do?" Marc asked Ignacia.

"Yeah, just go up to her and ask her the same stuff you

asked me." She said as she struggled to pull her pants on. "I don't even know what she looks like." She continued as she pulled her shirt over her head.

"Well she's taller than me. Long brown hair, and a cute face." Marc said. John looked at Marc and laughed.

Ignacia climbed out of the car with clothes that made her look a bit aggressive; baggy pants, studded belt, black Filas with white laces, loose green shirt that read 'frijolera', and a black baseball cap with her ponytail sticking out the back.

"You're going to wear that?" John asked as she passed him.

"Screw you." She said in a cheery voice as she walked toward the stadium where the bus was now slowing down.

John smiled as she walked away.

"You want her, you bastard." Marc said with a big grin. John laughed and kicked the floor with embarrassment like a child.

"Yeah, she's sweet." John said.

"What the hell do you mean 'sweet'?" Marc asked.

"She is sweet. I know she said 'screw you' to me just now, but I know she's a special one." John replied.

"If you say so." Marc said confused. John looked at Ignacia leave.

"Plus, she is hot." John said. They both began to laugh.

Tall, tall, tall, tall, Ignacia thought as she saw the passengers of the bus get off one at a time. Finally she saw a tall woman get off. She began to approach the tall woman but stopped when she saw her stop and wait for the man behind her. *Oh crap! That must be her boyfriend,* she thought as the tall woman hugged the man who was just as tall. *Damn, they are like oak trees,* Ignacia thought as she watched them hug. *Well I guess I should get this crap over with,* she thought to herself as she began to walk toward the couple.

"Well hi," Ignacia said as she approached them. "I'm Ignacia Castillo, and I have a few questions for . . ." she stopped and raised her hand to the woman as if she were presenting her.

"Oh, my name's Amber, Amber Mangiardi." The woman said finally.

"So what's this about?" the man asked.

"Well it's just a quick little survey for your . . . girlfriend?" Ignacia said awkwardly.

"She's my fiancé." The man said. Amber showed Ignacia the ring.

"Well the survey is based mainly on personal questions." Ignacia explained.

"Well that's fine, Craig and I don't keep things from each other." Amber said.

"Very well. Have you noticed any changes in your body in the last few months?" Ignacia asked abruptly.

"Craig, honey, we'll be over here." Amber said cheerfully with slight discomfort in her voice.

"Hey Stewart," a man said from the bus. Amber's fiancé turned around, "the other bus stopped on the other side of the stadium. Can you tell them where we are?"

"I'm on it." Craig said as he turned to face Amber and Ignacia. "Well ok then baby, I'll be back soon." He kissed her and jogged to the other side of the stadium.

"Ok, he won't be gone long so make these questions fast." Amber said franticly as she pulled Ignacia behind the bus.

"Ok, there is no survey, I'm sure you know, but I do have to ask one question. Do you have any 'special talents'?" Ignacia said in almost a whisper. Amber looked around.

"Do you?" she asked Ignacia. Ignacia raised one hand. Amber stared at it for a while, and then it seemed to spontaneously combust then return to normal.

Amber jumped back in surprise.

"Jesus Christ, I thought you were going to have something like mine, but your thing is gnarly." Amber said.

"Well what can you do?" Ignacia asked.

"Well I can't spit fire but I can do this; do you see that tree over there?" Amber pointed across the street to a lone tree by a building.

"Yeah, what about it?" Ignacia said. Then, in an instant, the tree grew taller and small shrubs grew around it. "Wow, the guys will not be impressed with the whole 'flower power' thing."

"Why not? Wait, what guys?" Amber said. Ignacia turned to Amber and answered.

"The guys by the two mustangs over there." Ignacia said. She pointed at her and John's cars. Amber turned to look at the cars.

"Do they do anything?" Amber asked. "Well the guy pacing back and forth copies your abilities. And the cute guy leaning against the red mustang does electricity," Ignacia answered.

"Why are you guys looking for me?" Amber asked.

"Well we're not just looking for you, Amber. We're looking for about six other people like us." Ignacia explained.

"Where are these other people at? Are they here in Brazil?" Amber asked.

"Well no. Only Marc, the guy pacing, knows." Ignacia said as she pointed to Marc. Amber looked at him. Ignacia looked at her and asked "Do you want to go talk to them?"

Amber looked at Ignacia and said "Sure, but let's make this fast because Craig won't be gone long." Ignacia nodded. They both began to walk away.

"What is wrong with you? Just sit down." John yelled to Marc from the rear of Ignacia's car. John was trying to look nonchalant as he saw Ignacia approach, but Marc's nervous pacing made him nervous as well.

"Guys, this is Amber Mangiardi," Ignacia said as she presented Amber to the boys, "Amber, this is Marc and John."

"Hey, just remember that the most important thing to remember is that I'm John." John joked as he shook Amber's hand.

"Hey." Marc said in a very comical and awkward way. John tried his best to hold in his quip and laughter. Ignacia nudged John hard with her shoulder.

"Um, hey." Amber replied with a smile on her face.

"So what are we waiting for?" John asked after a long, uncomfortable silence.

"Right," Marc started, "well someone has to tell her, right?"

Ignacia looked down and John looked up at nothing. "Ok, I guess I am going to be the one to tell you." Marc said.

Amber replied "Well I'm listening."

"Well maybe we should sit down, because this is pretty heavy news." Marc said.

"If you say so. Lead the way." Amber said cheerfully. Marc wasn't sure he should tell her about the whole world being in some kind of danger. He didn't want a girl so beautiful to worry.

Marc led her and the others to one of the cars. He began to pace back and forth. *How do I put this?* Marc thought to himself.

"I'm sure you've noticed things." Marc said. "Like being able to do things that you couldn't normally do."

"Maybe I have." Amber said. She didn't want Craig to be aware of her changes. She didn't want to be written off as strange.

"What if I told you were special because of it?" Marc said. "And because of this, the world actually needs you to take initiative." He continued. "What would you say?"

"What kind of initiative?" Amber asked

CHAPTER 8:

ASSAULT

"So how are you adjusting sweetheart?" Craig asked his fiancé, Amber. She looked at him.

"I guess I'm ok." She said. Marc had decided to tell her the whole truth. After a few hours of trying to comfort her and helping her to come to terms with her purpose in life, she and her fiancé, Craig Stewart, decided to go on the pilgrimage with Marc. And now they were driving through an open highway in the middle of nowhere.

Ignacia and John were in the blue mustang. Marc, Amber, and Craig were in the Ignacia's car.

"Poor Marc," John started saying. Ignacia was driving. She didn't understand what he meant.

"What do you mean?" she asked. John flipped his seat from the laying position into the upright position to talk to her.

"Well did you see his face when he saw that Amber chick, he was completely in love with her." He said.

"Yeah I saw, but why 'Poor Marc'? She could still be interested in him." Ignacia asked.

"Are you kidding me? Did you see the huge freaking diamond on her? She's going to marry that guy and there is not a damn thing he can do." John said with anger.

"What is wrong with you John? It's not like it effects you." Ignacia said. John looked at Ignacia like she said something inconceivable.

"What are you talking about? That man is my brother, if he's hurting then I'm hurting." He said.

"Aw, you're like lovers." Ignacia joked. John laughed.

"Oh whatever Nacha." He said. They both laughed. After a few seconds, Ignacia noticed that John was looking at her. She felt she had to say something to break the odd tension. John had just noticed he was staring at her. Now he felt awkward.

"So what do you think they are talking about up there?" John finally said to Ignacia. He nodded his head toward the car in front of them.

"I have no idea, but did you see how she lost her mind when Marc told her what we were? She cried like a little girl. I half expected her to, all her kind do."

"Whoa now missy. Do you not like her because she's white or Italian or whatever the hell she is?" John asked in astonishment.

Ignacia scoffed and said, "No, I'm not racist but she looks like one of those rich, stuck-up, silver-spoon-in-

45

mouth brats."

"Uh-huh." John said as he laid his seat back.

In the other car, Marc was trying to get to know Craig. Marc got past his slight jealousy of Craig. After all, he had just met Amber.

"So where are we headed anyway?" Craig asked. "We've been driving for about two and a half days now." Marc thought for a moment. The night before, he had contacted The First and asked for their next destination. He had told Marc that London was the next best place to look.

"Well we're going to my house, in southern California, for a few days to know what our next plan is." Craig nodded and sat back. Amber was sleeping in the backseat. Marc didn't understand why. She didn't need to sleep anymore. *Old habits die hard, I guess.* Marc thought. They were now entering Delicious again. They weren't that far from home. Just a day of driving left.

"Hey, can you grab my phone and call John? Just hit redial." Marc said to Craig. The car was low on fuel and he needed to let John know he was going to stop. Craig grabbed the cellular phone in the cup holder and pushed the 'send' button twice.

"Hey John, it's Craig. Wait hold on a sec." Craig held the phone away from his face and turned to Marc. "What did you want me to tell him?"

"That I need to stop for some gas." Marc said as he looked at the fuel gauge. Craig put the phone to his ear again. "Yeah John, we need to stop for gas . . . Yeah . . . Ok." Craig hung up the phone and said, "They need some too. Apparently they were just about to call for the same reason." Marc pulled into a gas station and Ignacia fallowed in her car. They parked side by side at a truck stop that was virtually in the middle of nowhere, and surrounded by desert wasteland.

"Ten minute leg stretch. Wake Amber up. She may want to get up and stretch too." Marc said as he got out of the car.

As Marc got out of the car, he looked over at John and Ignacia as they got out. John was pushing buttons on his cell phone. He had been doing that an increasingly large amount of times lately. Craig stepped out of the car, fallowed by, a still half-sleeping, Amber. Marc walked to the trunk of the car and opened it. He reached in and pulled out a roll of Mexican currency.

"Craig, can you pump while I go in and pay?" Marc said as he started walking over to the store. Craig nodded. John started to walk in a rather swift pace.

"Marc, hold on. I'm snack retail." John said as he caught up with Marc.

"Damn, how do you say 'thirty on pumps three and four' in Spanish?" Marc asked as they reached the front of the line. The cashier looked up at them from his magazine.

"Therty on tree and four?" he said in broken English. Marc nodded as he handed the man fifty and a twenty. John leaned back and signaled to Craig and Ignacia that they can start pumping.

"So what do you keep doing on your phone?" Marc asked as he and John walked down an aisle, looking for food.

"What do you mean?" John asked as he inspected the back of a bag of pork grinds.

"You keep looking at it and pushing buttons." Marc said.

"Oh, Jake keeps texting me. I guess being a recruiter is boring work." John said as he picked up a bag of chips.

"What do you two keep talking about?" Marc asked as he pulled out bottles of water from a refrigerator shelf.

"He just keeps asking me where we are and crap like that. I just finished telling him like two minutes ago." John said.

Amber walked in. "Hey guys. I thought you would need some help carrying some stuff out." Marc smiled.

"Well actually I could use some he . . ." John began to say but Marc nudged his shoulder roughly. "Actually, never mind. We got it." John said almost instantly.

"Oh, well ok." She said. She looked at Marc and smiled as she walked away.

"Awe, does little Marky have a crush?" John joked as he paid the cashier. Marc laughed.

Then an odd look came over John's face, Marc noticed this and stopped laughing. Then Marc could hear a soft roar coming from outside. It was faint and distant, but it was getting stronger and closer. At one point, it made the whole store tremble. Then it began to fade again.

"What the hell was that?" John asked. Both John and Marc looked out the window and saw that huge sand clouds had kicked up. The owners of the other two cars, that had parked while John and Marc were inside, had ran into the store for safety. John and Marc ran out.

As the sand settled, Marc saw that what had made the roar was a giant ship. It looked like a giant, metallic mosquito. Only instead of six legs, it had two rear jet engines that pointed directly back, and two side engines that pointed back and down at a slanted angle. As it turned in mid-air, it slowed down and began to descend. As it came down over the street, the four engines simultaneously began to point down. The tip of each engine spread open like spider legs. It landed on these new legs. Then, the underside of the ship opened.

"What the hell is that thing?" Craig said as he grabbed Amber. Ignacia closed both her hands into fists. Marc looked away from the ship and saw her doing this. He was nervous too.

Two men jumped out through the opening on the side of the ship. Marc was trying to look through the sand that was still floating around. He saw that these two men weren't men; they were heavily armored soldiers. They had shiny metallic armor covering all parts of their body. Metallic masks covered their faces.

One had a mask that appeared to be some sort of horned creature; the brow of the mask was flat and it had three horns in a triangular formation. The mouthpiece looked like the mouth of a growling beast. The shoulders and upper chest were a dark gray metal; everything else was a silver color. He appeared to be a rather heavy man. Though most of his mass was in shoulders and arms. This showed he was strong, very strong.

The other man was the complete opposite. He looked a lot lighter and his mask was in the shape of an eagle's head. He was rather slim, even with the metallic armor. He was also very tall. But when he jumped out of the ship, he didn't touch the floor. He was floating inches from the ground.

"You think that maybe they are the reason that we're are sentinels?" John asked as he stepped back slightly. Marc thought for a moment as he saw the metal men still standing and floating in place.

"I don't think these guys are bad at all." Marc said. Then a voice came from speakers on the side of the ship, a voice Marc had heard somewhere before.

"Obtain all four subjects alive. Kill everyone else." The voice said.

"Damn! Never mind!" Marc said as he turned to Ignacia. "Tell them to call the cops or something!" he ordered. She nodded and ran to the store. Then Marc turned to John and said, "Well let's see how these abilities work." John laughed.

"Get Amber and drive as far as you can from here." John said to Craig. Craig nodded and ran with Amber to the car. They sped off in John's car. John turned and looked at Marc.

"Are you sure we can do this?" John asked. Marc nodded and looked at the two armor-clad warriors. The heavy-looking one began running at a slow and steady speed. Each step was like an elephant falling. The force of each step shook the floor. The metal man was speeding up.

"Marc?" John said nervously as he began to step back. Marc thought, fast, of something to do to slow down the human rhino. "I got it!" he said. Marc began to raise his arms as if he were trying to push something up. Then the roots of all the small shrubs around them busted through the ground at an explosive speed and grew at an unreal rate. The giant vines wrapped around the soldiers legs, causing him to trip and fall. The ground cracked under his weight.

The other soldier saw his comrade fail at his attempt and did a back flip in midair and shot out toward John and Marc at the speed of a bullet.

"John, can you handle that one?" Marc asked as he did the arm raising motion again as the heavy man started tearing through the vines. John didn't let Marc finish his statement. He was already running at full speed at the flying man. John jumped to catch him in midair. As John grabbed the flyer, he dragged him to the ground and pinned him.

"Hello, I'm John and I'll be whippin' your ass this evening!" John said as he slammed his palm against his chest and began shocking him. Marc was continuing to entangle the strong man. He couldn't keep doing this; the horned soldier was getting closer and closer.

At one point, the man was close enough to throw a punch at Marc. A punch from one of those massive metallic arms looked like it would take out an entire brick wall. Then, out of nowhere, a giant fireball came from behind Marc and crashed into the rhino-like man's face. It threw him several feet back. Marc looked back and saw Ignacia standing there with her hands out in front of her. He smiled and turned to face the soldier on the floor.

"Who are you people?" Marc demanded as he made more vines hold the juggernaut down.

"We are the AES militia. We have come for the human anomalies; you, Marc, and the girls." Responded the small flyer that John was pinning down.

"What are your names is what he means you jackass." John said as he shocked him once more.

"I am Apollo, and my partner is Hercules." The flyer said. Marc and John looked at each other.

"Are you human?" Marc asked.

"We were once but now, thanks to the good doctor, we are gods!" Hercules responded from the ground.

"Gods? Some god. You're tied to the floor with roots." John said condescendingly.

"There will be more, and we will be stronger." Apollo said. John shocked him one more time to silence him. Marc looked at the ship, which was idly standing in the middle of the street. Then, something popped into his head, something he should have thought of right away. *Is anyone else in the ship*, he thought. John looked at Marc and, as if reading his mind.

"Is anyone else with you or is it just you?" John asked. Apollo smiled.

"Attack!" Apollo yelled.

Hercules ripped himself from the vines that restrained him. Another man jumped out of the ship, he was as tall as Marc and running at full speed at John, who was on the floor wrestling with Apollo. The newcomer was also covered in chrome armor. His mask looked like the face of some sort of Greek sculpture. His knuckles were dark metal, like Hercules' shoulders and head.

"John, heads up!" Marc yelled as he dove out of the way of Hercules' charge. Hercules slammed into a parked Winnebago and actually crashed into it. The recreational vehicle flipped over and slid several feet.

John turned his head as he shocked Apollo once more. The third soldier was already diving at him. He tackled John off of Apollo. John grabbed his head and began to shock him with a massively high voltage level. The man didn't even budge.

"Meet our third member. Codename, Zeus." Apollo said. John was trying his best to push the heavily armored man off. But the weight of the man was too much. A small syringe-like needle came out of Zeus' right hand and pricked John's shoulder.

"What the hell was that?" John demanded from Zeus. Zeus let go of John and stood straight up. John inspected his shoulder. Only blood was drawn. Apollo began to laugh maniacally.

"What are you laughing at?" John roared as he got up and ran at Apollo. Apollo flew directly into the air; John began shooting bolts of lightning from his hands at him but missing. Apollo moved too quickly through the air. Zeus was just standing there, staring into space.

Then, in the same voice as Apollo, Zeus said, "DNA extraction complete."

Hercules finally jumped out of the flipped Winnebago. He ran to Apollo's side as he landed. John was running to Marc's side. Ignacia ran to John's side and checked his arm.

"I'm fine." John said to Ignacia.

"Guys, stay on your toes." Marc said as he saw the three metal men get into fighting stance.

"The ass that pricked me is mine." John stated.

"I'll take the flying one." Ignacia said.

"I guess that leaves me with the big one." Marc reluctantly said.

CHAPTER 9:

BATTLE

John shot a continues bolt at Zeus. Zeus returned the favor. The streams of lightning locked and both John and Zeus increased their voltage.

Marc was forcing vines out and forcing them to entangle Hercules and fling him around. Hercules continued to get up and charge, as if unaffected by the attacks.

Ignacia, in one leap, jumped to the roof of the truck stop. Apollo flew straight up and began flying around. Ignacia began throwing fireballs at him. She was missing, at least, two out of every three she threw. The ones that did land, hit him when he stopped and began doing a strange crushing motion with his hands. The hits made him flip erratically.

Marc grabbed Hercules with a giant vine and slammed him into a gas pump. The liquid spilled out and covered the cement floor. Marc had a brilliant idea as he saw the gas stop at his feet.

"Nacha, get to your car." Marc commanded as he ran towered John. Ignacia looked down at him and looked at Apollo. She didn't want to run from a fight, but she trusted Marc. She jumped down and began running to her car. Marc pushed John out of the way of the electric blasts. John almost fell as Marc absorbed every bolt without flinching. "John, get in the car with Nacha."

"But . . ."

"John, just go! I'll be fine!" Marc commanded. John stared into his eyes; he turned and began running to the car.

When John and Ignacia were both in the car, Marc yelled, "Go, fast and far!" Marc turned to face Zeus. Zeus stopped blasting electricity at him and took a step back when he realized he wasn't dealing any damage.

"Don't stop on my account." Marc said. "I thought we were having fun." Marc began running at him and grabbed him in a bear hug. He began dragging Zeus toward the puddle of gas. Hercules was shaking his head back and forth, trying to get the gas off his face. Apparently the gasoline hindered his vision.

"Apollo, I need assistance." Zeus yelled as he tried to fight his way out of Marc's grip. Marc was trying his best to hold Zeus but it was incredibly difficult. Apollo was watching the red Mustang drive away, then, he turned to the commotion under him. He didn't know if he should go after the two in the car or the one that received no damage from a direct lightning strike. Apollo began to descend to help his comrade.

By the time Apollo got down to help Zeus and Hercules, Marc already had his foot in the puddle of gas.

"Too late chump!" Marc shouted as a small spark shot out from his leg. Within a few seconds, the pavement shredded as flames blasted out from the underground tank; witch must have contained hundreds of gallons of gasoline.

As John and Ignacia were only shy of half a mile away, they looked back and saw a giant explosion. Shortly after seeing the massive flames rise and mushroom into the sky, the floor began to tremble.

"Jesus, we gatta go back!" John cried out as the sound of the boom caught up with the trembling. Ignacia, without responding at all, turned the car around. John looked down the other end of the road and saw his blue Mustang returning. *Thank God, they're coming back*, John thought.

As John and Ignacia reached the scorched earth that was once a gas station, Ignacia noticed that the people who were in the gas station were running off in the distance. She was somewhat relived to see they ran out before everything exploded. John was searching for his best friend. It was the only thing on his mind. Amber and Craig finally arrived. To Ignacia's surprise, Amber was driving.

"I thought you were driving." Ignacia said to Craig.

"But I wanted to come back." Amber said as she joined John in the search for Marc. Craig joined her without saying a word. They were lifting splintered wood and torched, metal sheets, one at a time, to check if Marc was under it.

Ignacia looked back when she heard a humming noise getting louder and louder. It was the ship. It looked untouched, and it was powering up. John jumped up and turned to it. All four engines blasted on as it began to ascend. It turned and flew away. But as it flew away, John heard something that, what he thought, sounded like another jet engine. It was coming from behind them. All four of them turned to see what it was. It was Marc!

His legs were firing flames at an intense speed. The flames began to fade as he reached the group. As he landed, the ship was already far off in the distance. Marc ran a short while when he touched down, to slow himself down. His pants were incinerated from the knees down. His shirt was in rags and he had cuts and bruises all over his chest and arms. The wounds, oddly enough, were beginning to heal.

"Thank God!" John said as he approached Marc and gave him a hug. Marc hugged him back and laughed. "You scared the crap out of me, man." John continued. Marc looked at Ignacia, who also had a look of relief on her face, then at Amber, who looked happy to see him still standing, then to Craig, who looked disappointed for some reason.

"How did you survive that thing?" Amber asked.

"Yeah, it doesn't seem natural." Craig said.

"Well," Marc began, "thanks to Nacha, fire won't burn me anymore."

Ignacia had a look of accomplishment when she heard this.

"Well it's great that you're ok." Amber said.

"Yeah, super." Craig said, almost sarcastically. Marc ignored the sarcasm as he turned to face John.

"I think it's a good idea if we leave. If I made it out ok, then maybe those things did too." Marc said to John.

"Yeah," John said, "no sense in staying to find out." John turned to Amber. "Hey do you have my keys?" She tossed them to him. Then all five began walking toward the two cars parked in the middle of the street. Amber and Craig got into the red Mustang. Ignacia stopped walking and turned to Marc.

"I am not riding with them." She whispered to him.

"Why not?" John asked as she handed Marc her keys.

"Because I don't like them." She whispered, now a bit annoyed. She got into John's car and waited for him.

As Marc entered Ignacia's car he said, "Well I have no problem driving this thing." John sat in the driver's seat of his car.

He turned to Ignacia and said, "Well, at least his cloths stayed on." She laughed as John began driving north. Marc fallowed close behind.

* * *

Shortly after the two cars departed, Apollo slowly landed in the middle of the street. He watched as the cars disappeared into the distance. He turned when he heard a commotion coming form the ruined truck stop. Zeus was digging his way out from under the wreckage.

"How did you survive?" Apollo asked. He noticed that chunks of Zeus's armor were ripped from his body. Part of his face could be seen.

"Just barely." Zeus answered. His English accent was now audible. "How did you survive?"

"The explosion shot me up." Apollo answered as he opened a small panel on his forearm and began punching the buttons that were underneath. "Where's Hercules?" he asked.

"I don't think he made it." Zeus said. "He was standing right over the tank when it went up." He reached for something in the wreckage behind him. "And plus I found this." he added as he held up Hercules's mask. "Part of him was still attached to this when I found it." The ship soon returned to picked them up.

"The doc won't be too happy to hear that." Apollo said as he climbed into the ship.

CHAPTER 10:

ADVENT OF A SOLDIER

LATER THAT DAY, MARC was in Ignacia's car, she was driving. John was in his car with Amber and Craig. For some reason, Ignacia did not want to be anywhere in close proximity to Amber or her fiancé. She just didn't seem to like her very much. In fact, she seemed to despise her. Marc and John had noticed. If Amber and Craig had noticed was anybody's guess.

"You don't mind if I go talk to The First, do you?" Marc asked Ignacia.

"Oh, go ahead. I didn't think you had to ask." She said.

"Well, I know it kinda creeps you out. I just thought I should ask before doing it in front of you." He said as he leaned his seat back.

"Just go ahead. I have to get used to it eventually." She replied.

Marc closed his eyes. He looked as if he had fallen asleep. Then, he suddenly opened his eyes, which were glowing a bright green. The glow of his eyes almost illuminated the entire inside of the car. He woke up in his living room, lying in his couch.

As he sat up, The First walked out from the kitchen. Marc rubbed his eyes as if he had just woken up from a heavy sleep.

"Hey Marc. What brings you here?" The First asked as he sat down in the couch across the room.

"We were attacked." Marc said simply as the radio in the corner of the room turned on.

"By who? What did they want?" The First asked franticly. The expression on his face went from relaxed to worry as he sat up.

"By some weird, robotic-looking guys." Marc said. "They wanted me and the other sentinels. I don't know who they were working for."

"How did you get rid of them?" The First asked.

"Well, me, John, and Ignacia defended ourselves. Well actually, I um, blew a gas station up, around them." Marc said in amusement. The song 'Stairway To Heaven' began playing on the radio.

"Well that's impressive." The First said. "But how could they have found you? That's the only thing that is bothering me. The last I checked, you were all in the-middle-of-nowhere, Mexico." The First did not seem to relax at all while Marc put his feet up on the sofa he was sitting in.

"Well that is what I came here for. I need you to kinda council me in this." Marc said.

"Well have you spoken to anybody about your situation?" The First asked.

"Well no one besides my mother and Chuck know I'm here. And not even they know about my abilities." Marc said as he began to think of how these 'super' soldiers even knew where to start looking.

"Come on Marc, there had to have been someone else who knew you were in that area." The First said sternly. The tone in his voice showed that the First was worried about Marc.

"Wait!" Marc said, almost yelling, as he sat back up. "I know who else knew we were out there."

"Well tell me, you moron!" The First said.

"It was an old friend of mine. John gave him a ride a few days back, remember?" said Marc.

"Where was the Luther kid giving him a ride to?" The First asked.

"He was going to this warehouse that was owned by Chimer-Tech. That's a medical corporation or something like that. They have their hand in a lot of projects all over the world." Marc explained.

"Well you seem to know a lot about this Chimer-Tech." The First said, impressed by Marc's knowledge of the company.

"Well they have been on the news a lot lately." Marc explained. "The son of the guy who owns the company went missing from his home. There has been a manhunt for him ever since."

"You think they got to your friend and made him talk?" The First asked.

"No, how would they have known to look for Jake unless . . ." Marc stopped as he thought of something. He realized something he should have noticed before. Jake was in another country with, what was supposed to be, a military vehicle. If that was so, wouldn't he have been in trouble unless it was for military purposes? John told him that Jake was there to meet friends. What kind of friends. And why did Jake want to keep in touch with John so much?

"Oh my god." Marc said. "Jake is working for them."

"Well," The First said, "now we have to figure out who *they* are. Do you know why these guys were after you in the first place?"

"Well the smaller one called us 'Human Anomalies', maybe they knew what we are." Marc stated.

"Maybe they are behind the disappearance of the twin sentinels." The First said. "Wait; let me see if any others have gone missing." He said as his eyes began to glow a bright green for a moment. "Well Gregory Gustav, your Rock Sentinel, is missing and so is Tobias Schmidt, your Wind Sentinel. Maybe they were the two that attacked you earlier." The First explained.

"No." Marc stated. "These guys were different. If they were sentinels, I would know it. I can kinda feel it when John, Ignacia, or Amber are around. And besides, if they were sentinels, why didn't I get their abilities?" He said. "Wait," he began to remember the third soldier, "there was a third guy. He had John's abilities."

"How is that possible?" The First asked.

"He did something to John just before he started fighting though. I think he took blood from him." Marc said curiously.

"Perhaps these soldiers are not sentinels but maybe they are meant to mimic them." The First said. "Maybe the person they work for was able to tap into the gene that allows them to use their abilities."

Marc began to wonder about Jake. "Oh God," he said to the First, "Jake really is working with them."

"Are you sure, Marc?" The First asked him. Marc was certain. He did not have to answer the First's question.

"John is going to be pissed." Marc said, trying to lighten up the moment, as John would have done.

"If this Jake guy knows where you live then I don't think you should go home. If they assaulted you at a gas station then what makes you think they won't assault you at your own home?" The First asked.

"If they know who I am then they know about my mom and step-dad. I have to go home and check if they are ok." Marc responded.

"You have a good point." The First said. "I guess you should go home. But I don't think you should stay for very long. We have to keep on the move. If they found at least four of your sentinels then they will find the final two soon. You must find them first."

Marc got up and began walking toward the door. He put his hand on the knob and stood there for a moment. Then he asked, "Where is the next one?"

The First looked at him and responded, "London. His name is Alexander Knightly." He smiled and added, "To find him easier, I suggest you get into a lot of big trouble over there."

Marc woke up and pulled his seat back into the upright position. The car wasn't moving. There was no one in the driver seat. It was dark. Marc couldn't see a thing outside the car. He stepped out of the car and began walking. The ground was made up of smooth cement. He noticed that it was not only dark, but also foggy. Where was he and where was everyone else? Why did the place seem so familiar to him?

"Hello?" He called. There was a faint echo, but no response. Then it happened.

BOOM, there was a lightning strike from one cloud to another just above him. He looked up and saw a few more strikes of lightning. The silhouette of one of the clouds looked like a horse of some kind. Then bolt after bolt after bolt began slamming into the ground in front of him. Marc jumped back and fell to the ground, as the bolts got larger.

First, I need you, Marc thought. And as soon as he finished his thought, the first appeared next to him.

"Dude, what the hell is going on?" Marc yelled as the bolts continued.

"Well your still in the Nexus." The First said, "I know exactly what's going on." He said as he looked up and saw the cloud that resembled a horse.

"Well should I be worried?" Marc asked as he stood up. He still squinted as each bolt of lightning crashed down.

"No," The First said calmly, "but you should be relieved. John, the Luther kid, is about to reach his full potential. You might want to tell him. Considering he may lose control for a few moments."

As the First finished his statement, Marc woke up beside Ignacia.

"Pull over!" he yelled. She immediately pulled to the curb. Marc jumped out of the car and ran into middle of the street. He began waving his arms to signal to John. John slowed his car to a halt a few feet from Marc.

Marc ran to the door and opened it.

"John, you gatta get out of the car!" Marc said

franticly.

"What's wrong man?" John asked as he stepped out of the car.

Marc couldn't answer in time. John's eyes began to flicker with electricity. Then he began to lose his balance. He was stumbling around so much that he had to grab on to the car to keep from falling.

"Crap, we gatta get far away from everyone for a second." Marc said as he grabbed John and began running. John tried to run along side Marc but was stumbling too much. Marc was pretty much dragging his best friend away from the rest of the group. Luckily, they were still in the desert somewhere, so they just ran away from the road and into the desert.

"Stay there!" Marc yelled as he saw Ignacia try to fallow them. John was starting to send out sparks of electricity. With every step they took, John let out more and more sparks. Each spark was getting bigger and more violent.

"Just hold it, John." Marc said as they ran further and further. John simply nodded. He couldn't answer; just groan.

At one point, John couldn't run anymore. He dropped to his knees and began to whisper something to himself. Marc leaned in to hear what he was saying. John was praying.

"As I walk through the valley of the shadow of death, I shall fear no evil." John said as he clutched the cross around his neck. Marc put his hands on John's shoulders.

"You're going to be ok." Marc told him.

"Oh God it hurts. It hurts so. . ." John stopped in mid-sentence. " . . . AAHHH!" He began to scream. His arms open, fists clenched, as he screamed into the sky.

It was cloudy. It looked as if it were about to rain. Marc took a few steps back. He felt a force gathering in the clouds above them. Then, a massive bolt of lighting shot not from the sky, but from John. It flew into the sky and slammed into the clouds. Causing them to spiral and separate.

The vortex of clouds was lit up like a spot light. The source of the light was a mystery to Marc as he looked up and saw it pouring through the center of the cloud vortex. Then thunder was heard, but no lightning. As Marc heard the thunder repeating over and over again, he realized it wasn't thunder, but something else.

Marc concentrated on the center of the light. It was difficult; the light was so bright. Then he saw a massive Clydesdale running straight down toward John.

It was larger than a normal horse, at least ten feet tall. It was a light shade of blue with a white main. It was running furiously on nothing. It was going faster and faster with every stomp of its hoofs. The thundering sound came from his hoofs. It looked magnificent to Marc. John couldn't move. Then, as it slammed into John, it exploded into a storm of blue sparks that floated around John for a moment.

The sparks looked like small stars. Then they flew into John through his eyes. As each one entered, John learned a new ability, and with it, the knowledge of how to use it. He felt the charge that stimulated his impulses increase a thousand times. Then he felt his powers explode into an uncontrollable frenzy.

Bolts of lightning flew out of John and slammed into the ground miles away. Enormous bolts that splintered Joshua trees and shattered boulders. The vortex of clouds stopped and returned to normal. Marc was trying to calm John down in order to stop the blasts of lightning that were flooding out of his body.

"John," Marc began as he put his hands on John's shoulders, "you have to listen to me. Calm down. You know that the powers are yours to control and not the other way around."

John began to shake his head. "It's different this time." He said. "Now I feel that . . . that monster kicking around inside me. Inside my mind."

"Well show it who is in control." Marc responded. "Make it listen to you, John. It is your beast to conquer. Don't let it own you!" He continued to say.

Finally, John began to yell like he was relinquishing a battle cry. The bolts of lightning stopped almost immediately, but John continued to yell. Then he simply passed out. Marc picked him up and threw John over his shoulders. *Now your going to make me carry you back,* Marc thought as he began walking. He knew it would be something John would say.

"What the hell just happened?" Craig asked in an infuriated manner. Amber was trying to silence him. She was pulling at his arm, and saying something Marc couldn't hear as he approached.

"Calm down." Marc said as he walked toward Ignacia's car. "It's under control now."

"You call that crap 'under control'?" Craig said as Marc and Ignacia put John in the passenger seat of her car.

"Look," Ignacia started, "I understand you don't trust people that you just met two days ago, but you have to trust us. If it weren't for us, then those chrome freaks we met earlier probably would have abducted you and maybe even, I don't know, killed you because you're useless to them!" She shouted.

Craig looked back at Amber. He was completely enraged. Amber said nothing; she got back into the car. He was angry to see she didn't try to defend him.

"Are you going to let this bitch talk to me like that?" He said to her. Marc quickly grabbed Ignacia by the arm when he saw her jolt forward toward Craig. Without looking at Marc, she stopped her advance and unclenched her fists, which were shaking.

Amber was saying something to Craig, as he leaned into the car. Craig looked as if he was going to say something but he held it back.

"Nacha," Marc said, "I know you hate the guy, he pisses me off too, but if we want his girlfriend to come with us, we need to bring him along. Please understand."

"I know, but do we really need to keep her around? You already have her ability, why do we still need her?" Ignacia asked.

Marc answered, "Because we may get attacked again and there is safety in numbers. And besides, they may attack her."

"Yeah, whatever." Ignacia said as she rolled her eyes at him. "I'm going to check on John" she said, then walked toward the John.

Marc leaned against Ignacia's back bumper and watched Amber and Craig squabble. Finally, Craig walked to the passenger side of John's car and just before getting in he said, "Well come on then, let's get the hell out of here."

Marc looked back and saw that John had woken up. "John," Marc called, "are you alright man?"

"I'll be ok. But I think a giant Budweiser horse just ran into me, or something like that." John joked.

"Are you ok to drive?" Marc asked.

"No but I can keep Nacha company. I'm still kinda dizzy, so I'll just lay back for the rest of the ride." John responded.

Marc nodded and walked to John's car. As he approached the car, Craig got out of the front seat and sat in the back seat; Amber got into the front seat. As she did this, Craig looked infuriated. Marc didn't care how Craig felt at this point.

"Well we're on the move again." Marc said as he got into the drivers seat. Craig said nothing. Amber sat with her arms crossed as she looked out the window. She looked both tired and annoyed.

"Ok, nice tension." Marc said as he began to drive.

"I'm sorry Marc," Amber said, "Craig is being unreasonable."

"I'm not being unreasonable." Craig said. "I just don't know why we should trust people who are blowing up gas stations, being chased by metal psychos, and having giant animals running into them from the sky and exploding!"

"Yeah, and it's barely Tuesday." Marc said, trying to calm the arguing couple.

Amber giggled, but Craig scoffed and leaned back.

"Mister funny man." Craig said under his breath. It sounded sarcastic. But Marc ignored it. He had enough of Craig's ignorance. He didn't understand why Craig couldn't just trust them.

CHAPTER 11:

SNAGS

"WHERE IS AMBER?" CRAIG asked as John and Marc entered the motel room. Marc just collapsed on the couch and pretended to fall asleep. So, unfortunately for Craig, John answered.

"Well some Mexican bandits came and kidnapped her. Now they will either sell her into slavery or hold her for ransom." John said as he walked across the room into the bathroom.

"Are you kidding? Is he kidding?" Craig asked John and Marc in confusion.

"Jesus Christ, man." Marc said as he sat up.

"Could we not use his name like that?" John said from behind the bathroom door.

"Look Craig," Marc started saying as he ignored John's request, "I understand you care about your girlfriend, but come on. We have things under control, ok? Christ!"

"What the hell did I say a-hole!" John yelled from the bathroom.

"Hey, if you had things so under control, then what the hell happen the other day at the gas station?" Craig argued.

"It was a snag that, as you can see, we took care of!" Marc said.

"A snag, a snag? That was a snag? I can't wait to see what the real threat is." Craig said as he sat down on the other bed rather roughly.

"Listen, douche bag, if you don't like the way we handle things then get the hell out!" John said as he walked out of the bathroom. "None of us asked *you* to come along. We asked your little fiancé in the other room to come along, not you. You are the one that decided to come along."

Craig sat there for a moment. He didn't know what to say. Marc didn't know what to say. Finally, Craig laid back and said, "I came because I wanted to be sure she was ok."

"That's not true." Marc said as he stood up.

"What do you mean? Of course it is." Craig responded.

"Look," Marc said, "I've only known Amber for a week but even I know that she can take care of herself. But the beauty of this trip is that she won't be by herself. You saw how we handled ourselves the other day. We'll take care of her. So tell me, why are you really here?" When Marc looks for information, he always gets it.

"I love her. Why else would I be here?" Craig said. "I wanna make sure she is ok. And that is the truth."

Marc knew, deep down inside, that really was the truth.

"You love her?" John asked. Marc knew that there was more coming. "Dude, your such a fag." John said as he walked towards the door.

Then, Marc saw something that he didn't think he would see; Craig smiled. The tension was broken and Marc could now relax.

"Hey, where do you think you're going?" Marc asked John when he noticed he was leaving.

"Oh, Nacha and I want to go check out the town. It's not often we're in TJ." John said.

"So what? You're not going to ask if we want to go or what?" Marc asked.

"Well we were going to get to know each other a little more, you know?" John said a bit awkwardly.

"Jesus, and you called me a fag." Craig said as he lay back with a slight laughter. John looked at Craig for a moment.

"Shut up." John said to Craig, and then walked out. Marc laughed and turned to Craig.

"Listen man, I know how you feel. But you don't have to worry about us taking care of her. You can trust us, ok?" He said to Craig.

Craig remained silent for a while. "I'd still like to tag along if you don't mind." He said.

"No problem man. Just try to keep the criticism to a minimal." Marc said as he reached for his bag, which was leaned against the couch. He laid it on his lap and began to search through it.

Craig sat up and looked at Marc. "What room are the

JONATHAN LOPEZ

girls staying in?" He asked Marc.

"Um, room eight. It's right next door." Marc responded as he pulled a phone card out of his bag. As he did, Craig stood up and walked toward the door.

"I think I'm going to apologize to Amber for acting like a jackass. And maybe tell her we're friends now." Craig said. "Who are you ganna call?" He asked Marc as he opened the door.

"Ghost busters." Marc joked as he grabbed the phone. Craig laughed and walked out.

Marc began to punch the code on the phone card into the phone. Than he punched in his mother's home phone number. It rang for a moment but there was no answer. He looked at the clock on the wall; it read 1:07 am. *Well no wonder she didn't answer.* Marc thought to himself. He left her a message and hung up the phone. The he picked up the phone again and dialed the code again, but this time he punched in Camille's house number. He knew John forgot to call her. It rang for a moment.

"Hello?" Camille said as she answered the phone.

"Hey Cam. It's Marc." Marc said as he sat back in the couch. "I'm not bothering you right now, am I?" he asked.

"Actually no." Camille said as her voiced relaxed. "I just got home from work."

"Oh really? Who was watching Sabi?" Marc asked

"Your mom and dad volunteered. Well your mom did at least." Camille joked.

"I figured." Marc said with a smirk.

"So how is my knuckle-head of a brother?" Camille asked.

"Oh you know him. He met a girl." Marc said. He was

74

expecting an angry response from Camille.

"Wow, did he flip her and leave her?"

"Actually, I think she might actually be his first official girlfriend." Marc said in astonishment.

"How do you figure that?"

"Well they're out on a date . . . I think." Marc said.

"You guys are taking her with you?" Camille asked.

"Well actually, we need to." Marc said. "But there is a problem with that." He added as he realized a problem they had all overlooked. Could Ignacia go into the US?

"What's the problem?" Camille asked.

"I don't think we can take her across the border." Marc said. "She's a Mexican citizen."

"Well I can run this by your dad if you want." Camille offered.

"No, it's ok." Marc said as he began to think of a plan. "Well I'll let you go, Cam. You should get some sleep."

"Ok Marc. But be careful." Camille pleaded. "I heard on the news that some psychos blew up a gas station a few days ago."

Marc laughed and hung up. He jumped onto one of the beds and turned on the TV. He began flipping through channels and stopped on the news. The image on screen was an aerial view of, what looked like, a crater. He lay back in the bed and got comfortable. He only understood half of what the newscaster was saying: terrorists, assault, group, travelers, American, and Mustangs. That last part got Marc's attention. He sat up attentively. Then the worst possible thing happened. The newscaster held up a police sketch of what one of the terrorists looked like. It was a sketch of Marc. He stood up and looked out the window.

He had a feeling that someone would come looking for him soon.

A few moments had passed, Marc dropped back onto the bed. There was a knock at the door. Marc stood back up slowly.

"Who is it?" He asked as he approached the door.

"It's Craig and Amber." Craig said from behind the door.

Marc opened and let them both in.

"Did you see the news?" Amber asked with shock still in her eyes.

"Yeah. What kind of crap is this?" Marc asked. "Those robo-bastards come in and start breaking crap and I get blamed!"

"Calm down. We just gatta get the hell out of dodge." Craig said.

"How far are we from the border to California?" Marc asked.

"We are pretty close to it. It's a few hours away." Amber said.

Marc picked up the phone again.

"Who are you calling?" Amber asked.

"John, he has my cell phone. We gatta leave now if we don't want to run into any more snags." Marc said.

"Hello." John said as he answered the phone.

"Johnny boy, come back man. We gatta leave now." Marc said. He hung up before John could answer. "Ok," Marc said to Amber and Craig, "pack up, we have to go."

Craig grabbed his bag and started closing all the pockets. Amber ran back to her room and, after a few moments, came back. Marc started packing all of John's stuff up for him. The blue mustang can be heard returning. After a few moments John walked in with Ignacia.

"Ok, we're back. What's the problem?" John asked as he sat down on the couch.

"Mexican government thinks I'm a terrorist and are going to arrest all of us because they think we are a group of said idealists." Marc answered without missing a beat.

John jumped back up and casually said, "I'll start the car."

"I'll start mine." Ignacia said as she fallowed John out of the room.

Marc and everyone walked out of the motel room as casually as could be. The two cars pulled up. Craig and Amber climbed into John's car. As Marc approached Ignacia's car he looked at the front office of the motel. He could see the clerk through the oversized windows. The clerk was sitting behind his desk, watching TV. The clerk slowly looked up from the screen and stared back at Marc, and then he slowly stood up.

Marc threw his bag into Ignacia's car and jumped in. As both cars rushed out of the parking lot, John stuck his hand out the window and, instead of a jolt of electricity from his hand, a bolt of lightning crashed from the clouds above and into the power lines, causing a massive blackout. John looked at his hand in confusion for a moment, and then sped off.

Marc sat in Ignacia's car as they rushed towards the border. He tried to make contact with the First but in a new fashion. Only one of his eyes turned green and he began to talk to himself.

"First, are you there? Can you hear me?" he said. Ignacia turned to him for a moment. Marc shook his head at her.

[I'm right here] the First replied in an echo in the back of Marc's mind.

"Jesus! It works. Ok, is there any way I can talk to the other sentinels like the way I'm talking to you?" Marc asked.

[Yes, but there will be no restriction. One message you send will be heard by every sentinel you've been in contact with.] The First replied.

"I don't care, just tell me."

[Think of all elements you have under your control and *think* directly to the elements themselves. The corresponding sentinel will hear it. It works both ways.] The First said.

"You couldn't tell me this before?" Marc asked.

[Didn't come up.] The First replied.

Marc's eye returned to normal. He then began to think of fire, lightning, and bio. His eyes began to pulsate from green, to red, to neon-blue. He then turned to Ignacia.

[Can you hear me?] Marc thought.

Ignacia jumped and turned to Marc.

[Was that you, Marc? I can hear you in my head.] Ignacia replied.

[Um, me and Amber can hear both you suggers up here] John's voice came in.

[How is this happening?] Amber's voice echoed in.

[I'll get to that later.] Marc *said* [First thing's first. Nacha, can you go into the US legally?] He asked.

[I don't think that is an appropriate question.] John interrupted.

[Just answer the question Nacha.] Marc demanded.

[Well not completely.] Ignacia replied.

[What do you mean by that?] Amber asked.

[Well, I'm an unemployed Mexican citizen; I have no business in the US, according to your government.] Ignacia said condescendingly. She and John increased speed as the faint sound of sirens filled the night air. They passed a sign that read '2 miles to American/Mexican border'.

[Well we need to think fast if we want to make it across the border.] John said. Marc thought for a moment. Then an idea so perfect, but dangerous, popped into his head.

[John, call Jake up.] Marc said.

[Why him?] John asked.

[Just do It. Tell him to meet us at the border. Now!!] Marc shouted. He then severed the telekinetic line.

"Why did you want John to call your friend?" Ignacia asked as she increased speed. Flashing lights came into view in the rearview mirrors.

"I am under the suspicion that he is working with the metal freaks that attacked us earlier today." Marc said calmly. "He was the only other person who new where we were at."

"But why tell him where we are going to be?" Ignacia wondered.

"If they attack again, then officials at the border will see who is attacking and thus, putting them in the spotlight." Marc said. "And if a fight happens, you can slip through, undetected." He added slyly.

"You know this is dangerous, right?" She said, already knowing the answer.

"If you're scared, then let's turn back." Marc said, daringly. Ignacia stared at him. She was no longer paying attention to the road. He stared back at her. The car picked up speed. It was going faster and faster. They both smiled.

CHAPTER 12:

COYOTES

FINALLY, THEY APPROACHED THE border. There were several armored vehicles already barricading the road. Men stood behind several cruisers with their guns drawn. Both Mustangs came to a stop, side by side, several feet from the line. Everyone got out of the cars. Marc and John looked at each other.

"I think they were waiting for us." John said. Cars could be heard approached from behind. They were more police vehicles.

"What are we doing, Marc?" Amber asked as the officers cocked their weapons. They put their hands in the air.

"Just wait. It will be here soon." Marc said in

confidence.

An officer stepped out from behind the wall of cars by the border. He had a megaphone in his hand. He raised it to his mouth and began to talk.

"Step away from the vehicles and get down on the ground, now!" The officer demanded.

"Nah," John yelled back. "I like my car, and the ground is kinda dirty." This comical defiance was nothing new, from John.

"Get down on the ground, now!" The officer barked at them.

Nobody moved. The night was quiet. All that was heard was the wind picking up. Then, a roar can be heard in the distance. The same roar that Marc and John heard in the gas station. Everybody looked up, including the officers.

A light was visible above the clouds. It was getting closer and closer. The object was getting bigger and bigger. It was the ship they had seen before.

"There are your real terrorists!" Marc yelled as the ship landed. "Guys, when I say so, get back to the cars and get across that border and don't look back." he added while turning his head back.

They saw a large, dark figure jump out from the open latch on the underside of the ship. It crashed to the floor with a heavy thump. Then another figure jumped off the top of the ship. This one landed in the light.

He was taller than any of the other metallic soldiers. His armor was dark silver and gold. There was no face, just the eyes; which were gold. The entire face was covered in metal, like a helmet. And like the others, there was no skin visible. The entire body was encased in metal.

"Oh great! What's your name? Goldie Locks?" John

said in a backhanded tone of voice.

"I am Coronus." The figure said. The officers, at this point, had turned their aim to the shiny, new figure. "And this," He continued, "Is Hercules 1.5."

The heavy figure walked out from under the ship. It was the spinning image of Hercules; the metallic soldier they had blown up in the gas station. The only difference was that this one seemed a lot heavier than the last one, and it looked a lot stronger. Coronus took several steps toward the sentinels.

"Stop right there!" the officer with the megaphone barked. The officers just arriving from behind the two Mustangs were now drawing their weapons and aiming at the two metallic soldiers. Coronus stood still for a second.

Then Coronus said, "What are you going to do? Shoot me? But how will you shoot me," Coronus looked at the darkness that covered the desert. "If you can't see me?" The darkness then began to move closer to him. It got closer to the light. It was moving directly under the light. The light looked like it was bending. Before anyone could react, the darkness had covered everything.

Marc looked around and could see nothing. He thought for a second of what to do. There was audible movement in the shadows.

"Nacha, spark up!" Marc yelled finally. Out of the shadows there was a small spark then, a huge flame ensued. It was moving. It was Ignacia. Her entire body was engulfed in flames. But she wasn't burning. It was as if her body was the flames. Her body lit up the entire area.

"Fire at will!" one of the officers yelled. Ignacia jumped behind one of the cars. John began to bring down bolts of lightning from the sky. Each bolt lit everything up for a split second. In those split seconds, there were two shimmers visible; one was gold, the other was dark silver. The officers began firing at the metallic shimmers. The sounds of gunfire and ricochets filled the air.

John began aiming the bolts at the cars. It only took two bolts to made a car explode. The flames exposed Hercules' location. The officers began firing at him. He slammed one hand into the ground and began lifting the giant slab of earth that the armored cars were parked on. He flipped it toward the firing officers. They fell back as they saw the vehicles and giant rock crashing down toward them.

Then, out of the darkness, Amber dove toward them and forced several giant roots out of the ground. The massive vines caught the giant rock and cars. She made the root holding the slab of earth smash into Hercules. The impact sent him flying.

John had blown up several other cars and lit the area well with the flames. Ignacia had disappeared. Marc looked at John.

"Where's the gold bastard?" Marc asked. John shrugged his shoulders. John turned his head back toward the shadows. Then, in a flash of light, Coronus appeared directly in front of John, with his hand grasping John's neck. Then a fist-sized fireball flew from behind the red Mustang. It slammed into Coronus. He dropped John as he stumbled back. He turned to face the direction the fireball came from. Ignacia was standing behind the car. Her body was beginning to catch fire again.

"Hit me with what you got, sweet thing" Coronus said as he got into his fighting position. Ignacia began running toward him. Halfway to him she burst into flames. Then she picked up speed like a rocket. She began to fly. Her fists made contact with his chest. He flew back. She caught him in midair and began lifting him into the air. He pressed one hand against one side of her stomach. Then, a pulsating, multicolored beam of light blasted from his palm. It blew through her side. She screamed in pain and dropped thirty feet to the ground. John jumped and caught her just before she hit the ground. Coronus slammed into a police car.

"You saved me." Ignacia said.

"Well hey," John said as he tried to think of something funny to say. "I couldn't let a half-naked girl get dirty." He finally said. He looked at the gaping hole in her side. She began to close her eyes.

"Are you ok?" John asked.

"I'm fine." Ignacia said. Her wound stopped bleeding. John carried her to the car. Then he turned to face Coronus. Coronus was standing on the hood of the car he slammed into.

"Awe, are you going to cry?" Coronus taunted John.

"You son of a bitch!" John yelled as he threw a bolt of lightning from his hand. Just before it slammed into Coronus, he was gone in a flash. And in another flash, he was next to John. John threw a punch and as it connected with Coronus' chin, a flash of lightning blew out of his knuckles. The blow made Coronus lose balance. John began pummeling away at Coronus. Each hit was amplified by lightning.

Marc turned to the officers and saw they were battling against Hercules. Amber was holding him with vines as the officers unloaded round after round of their rifles and automatic weapons. Each bullet was just bouncing off of him.

Marc then began running toward John and Coronus. As he approached Coronus, Marc's hands exploded into flames. He jumped toward Coronus, who was shooting at John with his arm that had just converted into some sort of canon; beams of pulsating light shot out of the canon. Marc tackled the soldier to the ground and began to punch him.

"John, take care of the big guy." Marc ordered.

"Why me?" John asked as he stood back up; he had dived to dodge one of the blasts of light.

"Because you are the strongest right now." Marc said as he wrestled around the ground with Coronus.

John turned around and began running toward Hercules. As John ran faster and faster, everything around him began to slow down. He could see the bullets as they left the barrels of the officers' guns. He could also see Craig out of the corner of his eye grabbing a gun out of the car of one of the officer's cars. John picked up more speed. Everything seemed to be slowing down more.

John then realized that he was still moving at a normal speed, at least to his perception. *What the hell is going on?* John thought to himself. Then he had a great idea. He raised one hand to the sky and a bolt of lighting came down. John could see as the lighting poured like a single stream of glowing liquid. He saw as it bent and twisted in its descent. As it dug into the ground in front of him, he grabbed it and was immediately pulled up. In a fury of light and sound, he vanished.

Then a bolt of lighting slammed into Hercules's back. Hercules was bashed into the ground. When the dust cleared, everyone saw that John was kneeling on Hercules's back, his fist pressed against Hercules's back. As Hercules began to get back up, John jumped up and disappeared into the sky via another lighting bolt. Then as Hercules began charging toward an officer, a second bolt slammed into his back. It was John again; and again, as Hercules got back up, John disappeared into the sky.

As Hercules began stomping toward the officer again he knew what was coming. As John began descending, a flicker of light warned Hercules of this attack and the mammoth warrior jumped to the side and John punched the floor with power. As John tried springing back into the air, Hercules grabbed him and slammed him against the ground.

"It's over!" Hercules growled at John.

"I need some help!" John yelled to Marc.

"I'm a little busy!" Marc yelled back to John as he struggled to aim Coronus's arm canon away from him as he lay, pined under him.

Then a shriek came from John's car; everyone was stunned. Ignacia jumped out of it, covered in flames. The only difference is that this time the fire was actually hurting her. Then a massive ball of flames fired into the sky. As the fireball plunged into the clouds, they began to spiral. The clouds began to turn into a dark-crimson. Then they opened. Everyone was dumbfounded by the site of the hellish sky and the burning red light shining straight down from the center of the vortex. Ignacia was the target of the light; she was burning and screaming on the ground. She was screaming profanities in Spanish.

But then she was silenced by a loud screech that echoed throughout the area; it came from the vortex. Then a giant predator-bird composed entirely of fire came rushing straight down toward Ignacia. Ignacia stood straight up and opened her arms in welcome of the beast. The inferno-raptor exploded on impact with Ignacia, and just like John's incident, she was surrounded by little, red, star-like sparks. After a small pause, the sparks rushed into her eyes; she screamed as this happened. But when it was over, she was crouched down. She began to laugh loudly and maniacally. Then she jumped and opened her arms;

an explosion, that threw even Hercules back several feet, erupted from Ignacia herself. Then, in a ball of flames, she took to the sky. After a few seconds, Marc realized that she was the Phoenix.

"Get to the cars!" John yelled as he jumped up.

Craig ran into the backseat of Ignacia's car; Amber jumped into the front seat and Marc into the driver's seat. John jumped into his car. Both of the vehicles sped off. Both cars and the blazing bird rushed past the border.

CHAPTER 13

M.I.A.

AS THE CARS SPED through the desert, Craig aimed the gun he took from one of the officers' cars. He was leaning out the window and firing at Hercules, who was charging behind them at full speed. Marc was channeling all the sentinels with the mental skill he had learned earlier that night.

[Nacha, what's the location on that Coronus guy?] Marc asked.

[I see him. He's right behind me. He's shooting at me] Ignacia said as she flew around the sky in her phoenix form. She did several rolls and loops in the sky to avoid the blasts from Coronus's arm-canon; two open slits in his back were shooting blasts of energy, propelling him through the air.

[Can you still blast at him?] John asked as he looked up at the dark, night sky and saw the blaze-bird dodging the streams of light that were fired at it. [Marc, we gatta help her!] John added. And without having to stop to think Marc had a plan.

[John, do you think you can take Hercules?] Marc asked as he veered of toward the direction of Ignacia and Coronus.

[Yes, but not for long. He's a smart one.] John said as he slowed down to get Hercules to follow him. John then took a sharp left turn; the car then started sliding sideways as John aimed one hand out the window toward Hercules. A bolt of lighting shot from his hand and struck Hercules's leg, causing him to trip and fall, face first, into the dirt floor.

[Maybe he's not that smart.] John said. [I think I bought you guys some time. It takes this guy a while to get up to charging speed. I'm on my way to help.]

Craig began firing at Coronus from the window. He was hitting him with almost every shot.

"You're pretty good with that." Marc said as he tried to keep up with the aerial maneuvers of Ignacia and Coronus.

"He's in a gun club." Amber said.

[Did she just say 'gun club'?] John asked. [And he's in the Peace Corp?]

[John, just keep an eye on that big guy.] Marc said.

John looked through his rearview mirror and saw that Hercules was starting to catch up.

"Are the bullets doing any damage?" Amber asked as she tried to focus on Coronus in the night sky.

"It doesn't really look like it." Craig said. "But he loses his aim on her when I hit him." He added.

John was firing another bolt of lighting at one of Hercules's legs but this time the giant soldier was jumping around; skipping steps and leaping to throw off John's aim.

[Guys, biggie is catching up!] John warned. [I'm ganna have to speed up.]

But Hercules was no longer concerned with John. Instead, he was rushing toward Ignacia's car. Then, Coronus stopped chasing Ignacia and started flying toward Ignacia's car as well. Ignacia did a loop in the air and started flying behind Coronus; she fired balls of flame from her beak at him.

[Guys, they have a plan. Watch yourselves.] Ignacia said.

Craig started firing away at Hercules to help John, who was hitting the iron-beast with bolts of lighting but unable to knock him over.

Then Hercules stopped running, the force of his speed made him slide several yards as he wound his arm back, then he slammed his fist so hard against the ground that a shockwave shot out toward the red mustang only. As the shockwave reached the rear tires of the car, the speeding vehicle lifted from behind. At one point, the ground was directly in front of the car as it slid forward on its bumper.

Coronus then sliced the car in half with a beam from his arm-canon. The rear half of the car launched forward as it burst into flames. The front half of the car flipped a few times and landed right-side up.

Now, because Ignacia has no solid mass in her phoenix form, when she flew straight into Coronus, he was engulfed in flames as she blew past him. Coronus dropped to the floor in pain. He slammed into the floor in front of Hercules. Hercules jumped over him. As Hercules was in midair, John forced a giant lightning bolt down on him from the sky. The force of the bolt smashed the metallic monstrosity onto his partner.

John stopped the car by the front half of the demolished car. He jumped out of the car and rushed over to it.

[Are they ok?] Ignacia asked.

[I don't think I could talk to you like this if they weren't.] John said as he reached the car.

[Sorry about your car.] Marc said as he crawled out through the back of the wreckage. Amber was pushing the car door open and stumbled out.

[Forget the car. I was going to sell it anyway.] Ignacia said with relief. [They're getting back up] she added as she flew over Hercules and Coronus; dropping two exploding fireballs onto them. Amber, John, and Marc rushed toward the remaining car. But just as they reached it, Amber stopped.

"Wait, where's Craig?" she asked as she turned around. Right then, she saw what was left of the burning carnage that was the rear of the car. Marc immediately grabbed her and started to push her into the car. "No, we have to go back! We have to help him!" she began to scream. "He might still be alive!" she continued as Marc sat her behind the driver's seat; John sat down in the driver's seat and closed the door, trapping her in the back seat. Marc ran around the car and jumped into the passenger seat. The car sped off with the phoenix overhead.

Coronus and Hercules got up. As Hercules started to charge, Coronus stopped him. He noticed that there was a city in the distance.

"We can't pursue them into a populated area. We can't risk exploitation." Coronus said. As he said this, a bullet hit him across the face; the bullet failed to penetrate the steel mask.

Coronus looked in the direction where the shot came from. Craig was getting up off the ground; he was replacing the clip of the gun. Hercules was about to charge at him but Coronus still wouldn't let him. The glass-like eyes of Coronus's mask began to glow as he scanned Craig. Coronus began to laugh.

"I think we may have found something else we were looking for." Coronus said while laughing. Hercules scanned Craig too and also began to laugh. Coronus pressed two fingers against the would-be temples of his mask and began to talk.

"Sir, we found a *Deus.*" He said. "We are bringing him in." He added after a short pause. "Call a ship." He said to Hercules.

Hercules opened a panel on one of his arms; exposing a screen of some kind. Hercules began to punch in a sequence of numbers. While this was happening, Coronus began to walk toward Craig.

Craig began firing round after round at Coronus. Each bullet connected with the iron-warrior's chest; barely scratching the metallic armor. Coronus grabbed the gun out of Craig's hands and threw it. He sucker punched Craig in the stomach, forcing him to his knees. Coronus crouched down next to Craig.

"So, you like to shoot stuff, I'm guessing." Coronus said.

"Nope, just you." Craig said as he caught his breath. Coronus laughed.

"Well we have people who can change that." Coronus

said. What appeared to be a star in the distance behind Hercules began to get closer; the ship was approaching. Craig sprang from the ground toward the gun. Coronus aimed one arm at Craig, but instead of his arm turning into a canon, a slit opened over his knuckles and a dart shot into Craig's side.

As the tranquilizer began to take affect, Craig saw the ship land next to them. Hercules grabbed him and threw him over his shoulder and carried him into the ship. While inside, Craig couldn't see who was piloting the vessel but he heard Coronus say, "Take us to see your father, Shriek." Then Craig lost consciousness.

CHAPTER 14:

BUILDING A SOLDIER

CRAIG AWOKE IN A daze. The room was dark. All he could hear was the quiet hum of unseen machines. All though he could see anything, he could still feel the room spinning. *What happened to me?* He thought to himself. He could feel himself pressed up against a cold, stiff table.

He had no memories of the last few hours. He struggled to move his arms and his. . . his legs! As he tries to kick his legs free, he realized he had no feeling from the knee down. At that moment, a light kicked on and exposed the contents of the room: a table loaded with what looked like surgical equipment, another table loaded with pieces of equipment that looked like they shouldn't be in an operating room, and what appeared to be the parts of a metallic skeleton on a stand. The skeleton was missing its legs. And there was a suit of cybernetic armor that looked to be modeled after a demonic amphibian.

Craig looked down at his body. His chest was open. The humming he heard earlier was coming from a device that replaced his lungs and heart. He no longer had any blood flowing through his veins; instead, he had a blue, glowing liquid flowing through tubes that replaced his veins and arteries. His legs were replaced by the metallic, robotic skeleton; they were still moving to his will. It is when he looked to his left that he began to scream.

All his inner organs were separately bagged and categorized in a cooled chamber with glass doors. They were set up as if they were in an invisible body. Craig began to kick and flail again; in an attempt to free himself.

"Let me out!" he screamed. "What have you done to me?" he continued.

The door on the far side of the room opened. A man walked in carrying a glass of water.

"Who the hell are you?" Craig shouted out.

"Oh, don't worry about who I am. Do you know what you are?" The man responded. "I heard you gave my men a hard time."

The man sat down. He put the glass of water on the floor, at Craig's feet. The man was dressed in a suit and had a white lab coat on over it. He appeared to be the same age of Craig's father.

"Who the hell are you?" Craig said in a more stern voice, clenching his teeth.

"You don't like being here. I can tell." The man said, ignoring Craig's question again. "You know, the others volunteered for this procedure. They wanted this gift. I will have to force it on you."

"What have you done to me? I don't feel human anymore." Craig said. His eyes would have begun watering if his body could still produce tears.

"Oh you still are." The man said. "I plan on changing that soon though."

"What do you mean?" Craig asked.

"Athena!" the man yelled. After a short pause, a woman walked in.

She was cover from head to toe in metallic armor. It was in the stile of Greek armor. She had a shield attached to her forearm. Her face was covered by a mask that looked like a more feminine version of Coronus's mask. Craig could see why she was called Athena.

"Athena here was a very skilled surgeon before the procedure." The man said. "I only altered her neural network. Her body still has its natural look under that armor." Athena took off a glove and showed her rather delicate looking hand; there was a hydraulic hissing noise as she took the glove off and put it back on.

"I downloaded Hercules's visual recording." Athena said to Craig. "That girlfriend of yours is my target. When I see her, I'm taking her out." She aimed a fist at the glass of water on the floor. A small slit opened over her knuckles and an arrow shot into it. The glass broke and water splashed all over the linoleum floor. Craig got angry.

"I swear to God, if you lay a hand on her I'll. . ." Craig said as he tried to pull himself free again; the man interrupted him.

"You'll do what? Avenge the people that left you on the desert floor to rot?" The man responded; Craig was speechless. "That's right. They left you there, alone, against my invincible soldiers. And you are still on their side?"

Craig was silent. He looked at the floor, thinking about what he just heard. He looked back up at the man and Athena; still silent.

"I know it hurts right now, but I can make the pain go away." The man said with a smile. "I can make you forget all the bad things. Because I want to help." The man walked over to Craig and leaned toward him to look him in the eyes. "You just need to do something for me."

Craig stared at the floor thinking about what he just heard. He thought about the fact that thy left him alone. He thought about how much Amber meant to him. He thought about his disbelief in her leaving him like that. Then he felt his heart break. He wanted to break loose to let it out somehow; he couldn't cry or move. Then he just got angry. *How can they leave me there like that? How can she leave me there like that? She said she loved me! Maybe she lied. Maybe she'd rather be with that Marc guy. I saw the way he looked at her.* Craig wanted to break something. He wanted to shatter something with his bear hands. He wanted Marc dead.

"What do you want me to do?" Craig asked.

"I knew you would see things my way." The man said with a smile. "The blue liquid flowing through you is a compound of blood and a altered gene that I found in my son. I don't know why it glows blue. It's your blood, and it started to glow when I mixed it with the gene. Some people aren't as fortunate to have chemical make-up like yours. Most of the soldiers must take blood directly from the human anomalies in order to take their abilities."

Craig looked at his open chest. The blue liquid was being pumped through his whole body. But unlike his original blood, he could constantly feel it flowing through him.

"What is the difference between what I had before and what I have now?" Craig asked.

"Look at the water all over the ground." The man said. "Can you see it?"

"Of course I can." Craig said. "Why wouldn't I be able to. . ." Craig stopped talking when he looked down at the water. He saw it glowing. "Why is it glowing?" he asked.

"I don't know, but only you are seeing it glow." The man explained. "I just see it as normal water."

"That's amazing." Craig said.

"What if I told you that you could do more than just see it glow?" The man asked. "What if I told you that you can make it do anything you want: freeze, boil, steam up, float, and shape into anything you want."

"How can I do that?" Craig asked; still mystified by the glowing water.

"Just think very hard about what you want it to do." Athena said.

Craig did as instructed. He concentrated on the water. He stared at it till he notice that it began to ripple. He wanted the water to rise up off the ground. The water began to look like it was boiling but it was just thrashing around on the floor, in a puddle.

Then droplet after droplet of water began to rise up off the ground. Each one was a different size. This continued until all the water from the ground was floating in a ball right in front of Craig's face. The man stood up and walked over to Craig.

"If you help claim what is mine, I will help get what you want most of all." The man said. Craig looked the man dead in his eyes, through the ball of water.

"I want to get back at them for leaving me there." Craig said. "I'll help you get whatever you want."

"I thought so. Welcome to the Pantheon, Poseidon." The man replied. "Let me tell you a story about two brothers and a gift."

Chapter 15:

Homecoming

THE SUN WAS JUST rising over the mountains in southern California. Nothing was heard in the streets or the houses; the city was still asleep. Few cars were on the streets, and they just breezed by.

Then, in a rush of sound and power, John's car flew down the street to the home of Marc's parents. It stopped in the middle of the street and the doors burst open. John, Marc, and Ignacia jumped out; Amber climbed out of the car, sluggishly. Marc began to knock on the door franticly.

"Mom, dad, wake up!" John yelled as he saw Marc pounding on the door.

"Nacha, go to the side of the garage and tell us what

cars you see." Marc said. Ignacia ran over to the side of the house and looked through a window.

"There is a blue SUV only." Ignacia said as she approached them.

"That means my mom is out and Chuck's asleep." Marc said to John.

"Well keep banging on the door. I have to go home and check on my sis." John said as he ran back to the car.

"I'll go with you." Ignacia said.

"Ok. Amber, you staying?" John asked. Amber just nodded. John and Ignacia just sped off as the door finally opened. Chuck Saw Marc and Amber with grim looks on their faces.

"Come in Marc. You too, miss." Chuck said as he opened the door to let them in.

* * *

The car stopped in front of John's house and he and Ignacia jumped out and began running toward the house. As they approached the front the door, it began to open.

"John?" Camille said as she walked out the front door with her daughter.

"Where are you two going?" John asked

"I'm taking the kid to school and going to work. What's wrong?" She asked when she saw the look on his face.

* * *

"What do you mean 'it's not safe here'?" Chuck asked Marc.

"I mean we are being followed and we gatta go." Marc added as he looked out through the window by the front door.

"Marc, what happened in Mexico?" Chuck asked as he picked up the house phone.

"It's a long story. But a man is dead and we might be next." Marc said as he ran upstairs. "Amber. Come up here." He yelled from the top of the stairs.

"What do you need?" Amber asked as she reached the top of the stairs.

"We are going to need a place to stay." Marc said as he opened the door to his old room.

"Why do you think I can help?" Amber asked as she stood in the doorway; Marc walked into his room and started looking through drawers.

"Because none of those guys know who you are." Marc explained. "They don't know your name, where you live, who your parents are, or even your age. So if we hide out with you, they won't find us."

"But I still, technically live with my parents." Amber said shyly.

"You're kidding me." Marc said as he slipped on a pair of sunglasses that he pulled out of the drawer.

* * *

"What did you guys do in Mexico?" Camille asked as she franticly packed all of her daughter's necessities.

"We didn't do anything." John explained. "It was these other people who were trying to hurt our friends and other innocent people."

[John?] Marc asked telepathically

[Go for John] John said as he walked out through the front door to wait for his sister.

[I think I may have found us a place to hide out but it means more driving. At least for a day and a half.] Marc said

[Where is that?] John asked as he noticed his sister, niece, dog, and Ignacia walk out of the house in a rush. Ignacia had the same look on her face that John did; this meant that she was receiving the same brain-transmission that he was.

[Amber's parent's house up in Seattle.] Marc said; even though it was a mental conversation, they could still hear the awkwardness in Marc's 'voice'.

[Her parents don't have a problem with us going?] Ignacia asked as she and John's family entered the car.

[No, they are in our Orlando estate for the next few months.] Amber said with embarrassment.

[I love rich friends.] John said as he turned the car on and drove away.

"So who's this?" Camille asked as she motioned to the women in the back seat with her daughter.

"Oh, how rude of me." John said sarcastically. "Cam, this is Ignacia, AKA Nacha. Nacha, this is my sister Camille." He droned. Ignacia reached over the seat and shook Camille's hand.

"Hi." Camille said. "How do you know my brother?" she asked

"We're friends." Ignacia answered rather abruptly. John, very quickly and discreetly looked through the rearview mirror at Ignacia when he heard this.

[Marc, where are we meeting up?] John asked.

[I think that the best place for us to meet up is the hospital.] Marc said. [I have to pick up my mom.]

"Ok ladies and," John paused as he looked back into his car. " Um, dog, we're heading toward the hospital."

CHAPTER 16:
CIVILIANS

JOHN SAW CHUCK'S CAR parked in the hospital's parking lot and decided to park right next to it. As John stepped out of the car he looked up into the cloudy sky.

"This is good." John said.

"Why do you say that?" Ignacia asked.

"I don't think I can perform well without clouds." John replied.

[Marc, talk to me dude, where are you?] John said as he began walking toward the hospital building.

[Pediatrics.] Marc said. [I can't find my mom.]

[I'm going in to help] John said. "Nacha, watch my

dog." He added as he began running toward the hospital. Ignacia turned to look at the elderly bloodhound in the backseat of the Mustang. But she then turned to look up at the stormy sky.

"Mommy, is there going to be lightning?" Sabrina asked.

"Maybe. It sounds like it." Camille responded.

Ignacia recognized the feint, thundering roar. She knew right away that it wasn't thunder. She looked down at the other side of the parking lot at John. He was looking at the sky too. He shot a look of worry at Ignacia and turned and ran into the hospital.

[Marc, we may not have that much time, buddy.] John said as he ran through the sign-in counter; the security guard was hot on his heals.

[What's the problem?] Marc asked. John caught a glimpse into several patients' rooms as he ran by them; they were all looking out their windows, toward the sky.

[Marc, they're hear.] John said as he finally saw his friend at the end of the hall. John suddenly stopped and turned around to face the guard. He slammed his palms into the security guards chest; a small spark flew out of John's hands. The guard flew back several feet and hit the floor; unconscious. Everyone looked at John in silence. John thought quickly on his feet.

"Everybody down. Now!" John yelled; everyone who was not in a bed or wheelchair dropped to the ground.

"Now, I'm only ganna ask this once: where is Marina Salazar?" Marc added.

"She's using the MRI machine on the fourth floor." A doctor said as he cowered behind the desk at the nurse's station.

John, Marc, and Chuck looked at each other for a moment. Then all three began running for an elevator that dinged open at that moment.

"Quickly. Out out out!" John said as he, Marc, and Chuck rushed the people who were getting off of the elevator.

When all three men were waiting for the elevator to reach the fourth floor they were just standing and listening to the music that was playing. This moment did not seem to fit their current situation. John saw his chance to lighten the mood.

"I hope Amber has cable." John said as he looked at the number by the elevator door change from three to four. The doors dinged opened. All three men ran out looking for the right room. Then they saw her standing at the nurse's station.

"Mom!" Marc yelled as he began running down the hallway. Then, a security guard leaped out from behind a corner and tackled Marc to the floor as his mother turned around. Marc tried to wrestle the man off, but couldn't. Then Marc sent hundreds of volts of electricity coursing through his own body to shock the guard without hurting him too much; the guard jumped off.

"Marc, what's going on here?" Marina asked as she ran to Marc. John and Chuck were trying to keep people back.

"Mom, we need to go, now!" Marc began to explain, but he was interrupted by a loud commotion from the far side of the hallway. Part of the outer wall had been blown off. They knew this because the space that was once occupied by a supply closet was now a rather improvised window. John ran to the gap in the wall to look out.

"Oh damn! Marc, we have a problem." John shouted back to Marc and his parents.

"Metal heads?" Marc asked.

"Yeah. Hey, where's Amber anyway?" John said.

"She wanted to wait in the car." Chuck replied.

"That explains why a tree is holding down Apollo." John said as he ran back toward Marc. "We have to get down there."

"Fine." Marc said. "Dad, I need you and mom to get to her car; I'm sure it's on the other side of the hospital. I need you to swing around and pick up Camille and her daughter."

"And Dash." John added.

"John, we're getting to the fight." Marc said as he turned to John.

"Marc, we're on the fourth floor. How long is it ganna take us to get down there?" John asked as they separated from Marc's parents.

"Come on John. I thought you had an imagination." Marc laughed as he began running toward the gapping hole in the building. Marc jumped through it and dropped four stories toward the ground. As he hit the floor his knees bent but he was not hurt. He looked up and saw John torpedo out of the building; John did a roll as he landed.

They both looked at the fray ahead of them. Amber was still in the SUV as she made a tree attack Apollo. Apollo was launching concentrated jet streams of wind at the tree from his hands. The jet streams sliced into the tree and tore parts of it off, but the tree was constantly pulling itself together and launching roots from under the ground to batter Apollo.

Ignacia was dealing with Hercules. She continued to

blast the floor with streams of fire so hot that it would shame a jet engine. The fire would melt the tar from the parking lot floor causing Hercules to get stuck. Hercules would have to smash his way out of these small tar pits as Ignacia pelted him with fireballs that shook the ground when they exploded.

Marc looked up and saw that the ship was hovering over the hospital.

"John keep an eye on that thing. If anyone pops out, take them down. I'm ganna go help." Marc said as he began to run toward the battle.

"So I don't get to have any fun?" John said as he looked up at the ship.

Marc stopped running and leaped into the air with enough force to push him over fifteen feet into the air; where Apollo was. Marc slammed into the flyer and took him down to the ground. Marc was pinning him down.

"Why are you doing this, Jake?" Marc whispered into Apollo's 'ear'. Apollo quickly threw Marc off of himself upon hearing this.

"How did you know it was me?" Apollo asked as he stood back up.

"Just a guess!" Marc said as he ran up to him and punched Apollo in the chest. The punch hurt Apollo but hurt Marc just the same. Apollo was knocked back down.

"How could you do this to us?" Marc continued. "We were your friends." Marc hit Apollo with a small bolt of electricity from his hand. The soldier dropped to the ground and writhed in pain as the electricity coursed through his body. "I should kill you right now." Marc said as he shocked Apollo again.

Apollo rolled over onto his back and reached for a panel on his forearm, and before Marc could react. Apollo had pressed a sequence of buttons and the ship was aiming a red light at Marc.

"Fire!" Apollo yelled. Marc looked up at the ship. A cannon had popped out from under the ship and was aimed at him. The cannon charged for a second; just long enough for Marc to start running for cover. The ship let out a blast that seemed too powerful for the manhole-sized cannon. Marc leaped at the last second and dodged the blast; that looked like a cross between fire and lighting. The blast hit a minivan that was behind Marc. The family sized vehicle was completely undone as only a smoldering crater remained.

Chapter 17:

God of War

A SOLDIER, WITH ALL black armor, dropped from the ship onto the roof of the hospital. And from the ten-story building, he jumped to the ground and landed with ease. The cement cracked as he landed with one fist against the ground.

His armor was mostly black except for his forearms and mask. His mask had no face design; he looked like a gladiator in every way. All that could be seen on his helmet were his eyes, his crimson eyes.

John threw several bolts at him, but missed as the soldier began to run toward Ignacia. John began running behind him but was not quick enough. The soldier tackled Ignacia to the ground; Hercules jumped in front of John and detained Him. John watched as the new foe made a large needle slide out of his palm. He stabbed it into Ignacia's stomach.

"No!" John screamed as a massive bolt of lighting crashed from the sky onto him and Hercules. Hercules was thrown several yards and crashed into a car, but John completely vanished into the light of the lighting strike.

"Aries unit completely operational." The soldier said as he let go of Ignacia and got up off of her. He stood over her as she clutched her stomach. Then the sky began to illuminate in a fury of light and sound. Giant bolts of lighting began to hit the ground just in front of Aries. John reappeared in the streams of light; he had a bright, blue glow around his body. He jumped out of the light-fury and started hitting Aries with blow upon powerful blow. Ignacia was already standing back up; her puncture wound had already stopped bleeding.

Ignacia turned to look at Hercules, who was standing up out of the wreckage of the car he had slammed into. Orbs of infernal flames began to form in her palms. The orbs appeared to be made of smooth, glowing red glass. They were the size of softballs and were burning the air around them, which meant that these orbs contained a high level of heat. She launched one at Hercules, who was already preparing to charge at her. People were running out of the hospital as the fight continued. The orb hit Hercules across the shoulder; the explosion that followed cracked the concrete floor of the entire parking lot. Apollo and Marc were thrown back several feet. But John and Aries continued their fight with little inconvenience. Hercules reappeared from the settling flames of the explosion. His armor was badly damaged, as he could no longer move his right arm and sparks flew from his chest and helmet.

Back at John's car, Marc's parents had finally arrived

in Marina's minivan. Camille, Sabrina, and Amber were rushing into the backseat of the van with John's dog. Marc quickly got up and ran toward Apollo. As Apollo began standing up, Marc ran up and kicked him in the face. Apollo's head snapped back and hit the pavement.

[Ignacia, how are you holding the big guy?] Marc asked. There was too much noise to yell it across the parking lot.

[I think he is fighting blind. He's done for today.] Ignacia responded.

[Ok, get to the Mustang.] Marc said as he forced roots from the ground to bind Apollo to the ground.

John and Aries, on the other hand, were battling in the middle of the parking lot. John threw a bolt at Aries. As the bolt headed toward Aries, he leaped to one side and shot a fireball at John. John let himself drop to one side as he let off a large bolt of lighting. Aries then leaped over the bolt and, in mid-air, he let loose a fireball the size of a melon.

Then, John did something unpredictable. Just before the ball of burning fury hit its mark, John turned into a body of pure electricity. The mass of energy disappeared as quickly as it formed. A blue shockwave pulsed through the ground and up the boots of the metallic soldier. Aries froze form the thousands of volts of electricity that were blowing through his body. As Aries was being electrocuted, a blue phantom emerged from the ground behind him. It was John. He was being re-assembled by electricity.

[John] Marc said. [Get over here] Marc was already at the Mustang with Ignacia.

John turned to look at them and then back at Aries.

"You got off light this time, machine!" John shouted at the still shocked soldier. "You won't be so lucky if I catch you alone." John then began running toward the car. He jumped into the driver's seat and drove off quickly behind Marc's parents.

"What was that about?" Ignacia asked as she buckled her seat belt. John looked at her from the rearview mirror and threw the car into a higher gear. "Aw," Ignacia continued. " You were defending my honor." She mocked.

"Shut up." John said, trying not to smile.

"You love me!" Ignacia said as she laughed.

"You suck." John said as he finally began to laugh as well.

Marc was glad to see that his friend was not being affected by the disasters that seemed to be fallowing them across the globe. He knew that with the assistance of his friends, and their support, this ordeal would be bearable.

CHAPTER 18:

NEW SKIN

THE ROOM RESEMBLED AN automobile's assembly line. Craig stood on a moving platform at one end of the assembly line. His body was a mesh of cold metal, tubing, and mutilated flesh. He was running one hand over the other out of nerves.

"Why doesn't it feel like I'm touching my hands together?" Craig asked. "It feels like I'm wearing gloves. Like my skin has no feeling anymore, but everything under it still does." Craig said as he opened and closed his hands.

"Well your skin has no feeling anymore." A voice said from speakers that were mounted in the corners of the room. The voice was of the suited man from before; he was in an elevated control room. "Now hold your arms out and put your feet in the locks."

"Why do you have to lock my feet into place?" Craig asked as a clamp latched around his feet.

"Unfortunately, I couldn't replace your whole body without you losing your abilities." The man responded. "So a result of that is that a lot of your pain receptors are still fully functional. Are you still up for this?"

"Yeah, I need this." Craig said after thinking for a moment. He held his arms out to his sides.

"Good." The man said. "Now, hands open and palms facing forward." As Craig complied with the last minute order, the platform began to move forward.

The first phase of the assembly was the retinal phase. A machine came down and surrounded Craig's entire upper body. Then he felt something begin drilling into the back of his head. As this was happening, two prongs stuck into his eyes and ripped them from his skull; Craig began screaming. Then a machine latched into the hole in the back of his head; the machine was really a small computer that was to never be removed from this point out.

Craig felt everything. He began to scream louder, but was powerless to the will of the machines. Something had locked around his wrists when the machine had covered his face. He felt something prickling down his spine. Then he felt something in the back of his eye sockets; it was like something was there but he didn't know what, they were coming from the back of his head.

Two bowl-shaped plates were inserted into his eye sockets. They covered his original sockets perfectly and each one had sensors and tiny electrodes along its inside. Finally, two crystal-like balls were inserted into each socket.

As the machine lifted from around Craig's head, he could see nothing but a lengthy computer code run. Then everything came into view like if he was a newborn baby; everything was blurry but slowly coming into focus. He was able to see with clearer vision and was now headed toward phase two of the process, the vital bone replacement. As the suited man watched the process unfold in front of his very eyes, Apollo entered the room.

"When will he be operational?" Apollo asked.

"Why so eager to have him in the field, Evens?" The man asked he began typing commands into a computer in front of him. "Do you want to show him how to fail me?" he added as he turned to look at Apollo.

"That last failure wasn't my fault!" Apollo immediately responded.

"Then I suppose I should make someone else the High General since you did nothing to help." The man said as Craig could still be heard screaming over the sound of all the machines that seemed to be ripping him apart.

"Just give me Shriek." Apollo said calmly as he turned to look at the horrific transformation that Craig was going through. "I believe he is ready for the field, and they will not be able to counter his abilities." Apollo added.

"You said the same about Aries, and now I have to recalibrate his visual systems." The man said as he began typing more commands in. "And who knows how much longer until Hercules is fully operational again." He added. "But very well. I will give you Shriek for one mission only. And you'd better bring him back at least at sixty percent efficiency. I can't afford to have his neural systems go offline."

"Thank you sir." Apollo said. "By the way sir, when is our next mission?" he asked as he began to walk out. He stopped at the door to hear the man's response. The man paused for a while as he watched Craig go through the final stages of the assembly line.

"After Poseidon's combat test." The man responded. Apollo then left the room. "Craig, how are you doing? Do you hate me yet?" The man joked as he spoke over the loud speaker.

"I feel fine. . . now." Craig said with enthusiasm. As the last machine moved from around Craig, it exposed that his body was completely metallic. All that remained was his face.

He looked taller and physically fit with the armor on. His armor looked exactly like Apollo's in every way except for color; Apollo's armor was chrome, Craig's was a darker shade of silver, also Craig's gloves had webbed fingers, and Craig's helmet was completely different.

As the machine that attached the helmet came down, Craig's arms were down at his sides and his shoulders were completely relaxed. The machine first latched the back of the helmet; the rear half of his head, and plugged into the small computer attached to the back of his head, perfectly. Finally the faceplate came down and covered his face; the faceplate was made to look like a cross between a piranha and a demon with a mouth-guard.

"Congratulations." The man said. "You are now truly Poseidon, my Aquatic General."

"I love how this suit feels!" Craig said as the locks around his feet released and he began to walk and move his arms around.

"Are you ready for a test run?" The man said as he walked into the room. He had a smile on his face.

"Yeah, I'm ready for anything now." Poseidon said. "I love this suit!" he said again.

"Good." The man said. "Well if you would follow me to the training room, we can begin your test run."

CHAPTER 19:

A LONG FLIGHT

IGNACIA WAS SITTING IN a window seat on the right side of the plane. John was sitting next to her as he watched people boarding the plane and take their seats. Ignacia had a look on her face that was a combination of annoyance and boredom. She turned to look at John.

"Ok, so how long is *this* flight going to take?" Ignacia asked as she yanked out one of John's headphones.

"Maybe eleven hours or so." John replied as he took out his other headphone and turned off his MP3 player.

"What? The last one took almost four hours!" Ignacia responded in an angry whisper.

Marc turned around and poked his head over the back

of the seat to face John and Ignacia. He had a newspaper in his hand. He showed them the headline. It read *TERRORIST ATTACK HOSPITAL.*

"Is that really appropriate right now?" John said sarcastically as the captain began talking over the intercom.

"This is your captain speaking. If you would all put all your seats in the upright position and buckle your seatbelts, we will be departing shortly."

As the plane took flight, Marc looked to Amber, who was sitting in the window seat next to him. She looked so depressed and sad. Her eyes look like she had been crying for hours. He wanted so badly to just reach out and hold her hand, but was repelled by the idea of it being too soon for her. After all, she had just lost her fiancé.

Amber could still not believe that Craig was dead. It was like some sort of nightmare that she could not wake up from. But there was this strange sort of guilty relief in the back of her mind. She never really wanted to marry Craig. The only reason she ever dated him in the first place was because he was the only boy her parents approved of. But now, she was free. Maybe that's where that relief came from. But still, she loved Craig; even if it wasn't romantic love, she still loved him. And his death was something to mourn. She then turned to look at Marc, who quickly turned to look away at something that wasn't there.

"Hey Marc, what time will it be when we get to London?" Amber asked. Marc looked at his watch and quickly did the math in his head.

"Well it's four o'clock now, and they are five hours ahead of us, plus it'll take us about ten hours to get there so. . . about seven o'clock tonight." Marc answered. "Why do you ask?' he added.

"I just wanted to know. And thank you." She answered.

"It's no problem." Marc replied. "Math was my favorite class in high school." He added. Amber giggled slightly.

"I meant for taking me along." Amber said.

"Oh." Marc said as he regretted saying his last statement. "Well I just thought we should all stick together, and plus, you've been to London before. You could help us navigate."

"Ok. And don't worry about your parents." Amber added. "They'll be safe in Seattle. I called my parents and told them that they will be staying there while their house is being remodeled."

"Good." Marc said. "The lower profile, the better."

As a few hours past on the plane, John and Ignacia were the only two still awake. They were having what appeared to be a marathon conversation about their abilities.

"But if you can turn into electricity and not lose your clothes, then why do my clothes nearly burn off?" Ignacia whispered as she pulled at her *Aguilas* jersey.

"I don't know." John answered. "But I think that night was awesome." He joked. Ignacia smacked his shoulder as she laughed.

"So why don't you just admit it already?" Ignacia asked. She turned to look out the window. It was morning already. The sun had rose a little faster than usual.

"Admit what?" John asked as he lay back in his seat.

"You like me." Ignacia said as she closed her eyes.

"I do like you. What do you mean?" John said. His voice seemed a little anxious. "You're cool. Why would I need to say I like you?"

Ignacia smiled. "Never mind. I guess I'll have to make

you say it." she said lazily.

"Say what?" John asked. But it was too late; Ignacia had fallen asleep. "I guess I won't be joining the 'mile high' club today either." John said to himself.

Later on, as they approached the airport, Amber poked her head over the back of her seat to talk to John and Ignacia.

"Ok, a few rules we have to go over." Amber said. John looked disappointed as she said 'rules'. "You can't verbally abuse someone in public, you cant touch those guards at Buckingham Palace, also, don't get into to much trouble, if the police find out her passport is fake, we are all screwed." John smiled as he began to think of something Marc had told him before they flew to New York.

"Hey Marc." John said, almost laughing.

"I know, John, I know." Marc said as he remembered the tip that the First had told him.

"You know what?" Amber asked as she turned to Marc.

"The First told us that we will have a better shot at finding this guy if we get into trouble here." Marc said. "So everything you just told us not to do, we're going to do."

Amber looked almost scared as she sat back down. Something about her seemed off to Ignacia.

"Are you sure she will help us?" Ignacia asked John. John just shrugged. "Rich girl, she might just sit back and make us find him ourselves." She whispered to John. John shrugged again. John always made a point to not judge people right away.

"Well we'll see soon enough." John said as they began to land.

CHAPTER 20:

THE PANTHEON

As Poseidon sat at his station in the cockpit of the ship, he couldn't help but keep looking over his shoulder at Hercules. Poseidon was intimidated by his size and ravenous-looking face mask. Hercules wasn't even looking in Poseidon's direction, if anything, Hercules could only see the monitor that was mounted directly in front of his face.

The ship was divided into three sections. There was the pilot's section, two pilots sat at the front of the ship, in front of them was a small windshield surrounded by monitors; their door was a latch that was located above them. The navigator sat in a small, square pit behind the pilots. The navigator was surrounded by controls that controlled the two monitors in front of him and all the monitors in front of the pilots; his door was a latch on the floor to his left. The pit was only two feet deep. Finally, at the rear of the ship, the gunner sat at the back. Now, the gunner was in control of the two machine guns on both sides of the ship. He had two monitors that showed him what the guns were pointed at.

Now if you hadn't guessed it by now, the gunner was Hercules and the navigator was Poseidon. The two pilots were Shriek and Apollo. Poseidon was having trouble doing his job properly from fear that Hercules would just decide to tear through him.

"Poseidon, can you bring up the world map on my bottom monitor." Apollo said. Poseidon could hear the voice in his helmet, like there was a direct radio link between the soldiers. The need for this radio link was to hear orders over the humming of the engines. Poseidon hit several buttons and switches on the control panel in front of him.

"And Poseidon," Apollo continued. "Don't let the big guy scare you. He's as harmless as a baby kitten to us."

"I know, it just takes some getting used to." Poseidon said. As he continued to watch his monitors and track their beacon.

"If you're ganna be scared of any of us, you should be scared of Shriek here." Hercules said in his surprisingly, normal voice.

"Why is that?" Poseidon asked as he turned his seat to face Hercules.

"Because Shriek here is more robotic that all of us." Apollo said.

"What do you mean?" Poseidon asked as he resumed his task.

"Because Shriek is the actual Human Anomaly that controls sound waves." Apollo said as he laughed slightly.

"But isn't that a good thing?" Poseidon asked.

"Yeah, but the guy didn't want to help us in the first place." Apollo answered. "So the Doc plugged a machine all along his spinal column and brain to make him listen."

"How did you guys find him in the first place?" Poseidon asked as he took his facemask off. His face was still the face of Craig Stewart but the rest of his head, including his ears, were still covered by the back half of the helmet and a small microphone stuck out from under his chin, over his mouth. And his eyes were no longer the eyes he once had; they were now blue, crystal spheres.

"He was the Doc's son." Apollo said with another laugh. "Hey, how far are we from our destination?" he said almost immediately after. Poseidon looked at his monitor.

"Were right over Ireland." Poseidon answered.

"I believe we should descend into the Troposphere." Shriek said in a soulless voice.

"Ok? But why should we be afraid of him?" Poseidon asked as he looked at his mask.

"Because if that computer goes out, and he gains self control, this nut will not hesitate to take us down." Apollo informed Poseidon. "Isn't that right, Shriek?" He said as he turned to look at Shriek.

"That is correct, High General." Shriek responded.

"Alright, take us into the Chimer-Tech facility outside Scotland." Apollo ordered Shriek. "I'd put that bucket back on. Re-entry is a bitch without it." Apollo said to Poseidon, referring to his facemask.

Poseidon put the mask back on. The mask responded to the helmet and latched itself to it with a hydraulic hiss.

The fit was airtight to allow Poseidon to submerge himself under water.

"Now entering Atmosphere." Shriek said.

CHAPTER 21:

CALLING ALL UNITS

THE YOUNG POLICE OFFICER was driving in an unmarked vehicle. He was wearing civilian clothes and speeding toward a stolen cab. He had one hand on the steering wheel and the other was holding the radio's receiver while he collaborated a plan with the other units in the area.

"Car twenty-three, block him off!" he said as he saw the cab turning right. Then a police car came from the alley that the cab was going to take and stopped at its opening.

"Now this road leads to a dead end, so I'll take him on foot." The young officer said.

"Knightly, are you sure you could keep up with him?

This guy was running for a while before he hopped into the cab." a voice said from the radio.

"Don't worry. I'm considered a bit of a runner myself." The young officer said.

And sure enough, the cab came to a screeching halt as the driver hopped out, it was Marc. He ran into a building. The young officer did the same and entered the building, behind Marc. The officer saw Marc run through a door leading to a stairway. Marc thought that at the fifth floor, the officer would stop chasing him, but the officer was still running at full speed. Every time Marc stopped at a landing to turn around and keep running upstairs, the officer would jump over the rails and get closer to catching Marc.

"Stop! In the name of the Law!" The officer yelled at Marc.

"Screw that noise!" Marc said as he kept running. At one point, Marc burst through a door that led to the roof of the building.

"You're an American!" The officer shouted as he chased Marc to the edge of the roof.

"Nice observation!" Marc said as he took a running leap off of the roof, toward a parking structure. When he landed, he rolled and had to get back up. When he looked back, he saw the officer in midair, coming toward him. Marc turned and started running again.

[Guys, I found him.] Marc said to John.

[How are you sure?] John asked.

[Because he's not getting tired!] Marc said as he leaped onto an incoming car and ran over it. The officer had no choice but to do the same to keep up.

"Sorry." The officer said as the driver opened the door

and stepped out.

On the second level of the parking structure, Marc leaped over a guardrail and landed on the sidewalk. The young officer didn't leap over the railing; he grabbed it and slid under it.

[I'm coming up on your location. I hope you guys are ready.] Marc said he turned down an alleyway.

The officer fallowed Marc into the alley and as he did, a wall of fire separated the alley from the street. The officer slowed his pace at this point. He saw that a large tree that was growing out from under the pavement blocked the alley at the other end as well. Marc turned down another alleyway that was halfway down the alley that the officer had chased him to. The officer saw Marc disappear behind the corner of the building. The officer drew his gun and started walking close to the wall. He was being cautious. He knew he was being lured into an ambush.

A fellow officer reached the opening of the alley, but was unable to enter due to the wall of fire. He was able to see the young officer disappear behind the building. Almost immediately after, he saw several bright orange and blue flashes; there were also splashes of water splattering from behind the building. After several minutes, the flashes stopped and there was nothing for a moment or two. Then, a man could be heard screaming as large blasts of water flooded the alley. The water put out the wall of fire quickly and the officer began walking toward the alleyway to see if his younger partner was fine. Then the screaming stopped

"Knightly?" the officer shouted around the corner.

"I'm fine." The younger officer shouted back. "I lost them." He stated as his partner turned the corner and saw him on the floor, sitting against the wall. The ground was still covered in water.

"What happened?" the older officer asked. As he saw the water all over the ground and the scorch marks along the wall.

"They had some amazing weapons." Officer Knightly said as he stood up.

"They?" his partner asked.

"Four men." Knightly said as he walked past him.

CHAPTER 22:

INTERESTING

"TOO BAD ABOUT EARLIER, Alex." An officer said to Alex Knightly, as he passed him on his was into the police station. Alex was off duty and headed out the door.

"Maybe next time." Alex said as he pulled keys out of his duffle bag. As he walked toward the parking lot, he saw a man and a women leaning against his car. He remembered them as two of the people from the alley, earlier that day.

"Ready to go?" John asked.

"Yeah, why not?" Alex said as he walked toward his car. Ignacia was reading an English to Spanish dictionary.

Alex opened the car and they all climbed in. John told

Alex which hotel they were staying at.

"How is your friend?" Alex asked; he didn't take his eyes off the rode.

"Marc?" John asked. "He's fine now. The question is if you are ready to hear what we have to tell you?" John responded.

"What happened to him in that alley?" Alex asked as they stopped at a red light.

"Well, when he acquires your, um, special abilities, he loses control of them for a second until he figures out how to flick it into off." John said.

"That's interesting." Alex said to himself.

By the time they reached the hotel, the sun had completely set. Then, John and Ignacia saw something disturbing; the clouds above the city were beginning to swirl. As Alex parked the car and the three of them got out, John looked at Ignacia and Ignacia looked back at him.

"It's Amber, isn't it?" John asked as they looked up into the saw the clouds swirl more quickly.

"Yes. What was her creature? I don't remember." Ignacia said as she began to breath harder.

"The Dragon." John said. Right then, they both looked at each other one last time and began running toward the hotel. "Alex, keep up man!" John yelled back. Alex began running after them.

They reached their room and John almost broke through the door as he opened it. They saw Amber crouched down on the floor, holding her stomach. She was moaning and groaning in pain. Her eyes were glowing a bright, emerald color. Marc was huddled around her, talking her through it. Marc turned to look at John.

"We gatta get her to the parking lot!" Marc said as he stood Amber up. "Amber. Sweetie, we gatta get you to the parking lot so that dragon doesn't blow through four floors to get to you, ok?" Marc said to Amber calmly. She just nodded. "Can you make it to the elevator without attracting attention?" he asked.

"I. . . I think so." Amber said as she straightened out her posture.

Soon, all five of them were walking toward the elevator. Amber was wearing a pair of sunglasses to conceal her illuminating eyes. As they made it to the elevator, Ignacia pushed the button to the lobby. As soon as the door closed, Amber fell to the floor again and held herself. All four of them huddled around her.

"By the way, Marc, this is Alex, Alex, this is Marc." John said.

"Nice to meet you." Marc said as he reached over to shake Alex's hand.

CHAPTER 23:

PANIC IN THE STREETS OF LONDON

AMBER RAN OUT INTO the middle of the parking lot. She didn't stop running until she reached a part of the parking lot that had as few cars as possible. The others were right behind her. Marc looked up into the sky and saw that the thick swirl of clouds was starting to glow green. The dragon was about to arrive at any second. People in the streets were staring at the clouds and some were staring at amber screaming in pain on the parking lot floor.

But Marc and John heard something that they dreaded; a roar of thunder was approaching from the northwest.

They knew right away that it wasn't thunder; it was an incoming attack.

"No, not now!" Marc said as he stood up and clenched his fists.

"Nacha, watch Amber. Alex, I hope you know how to use that super-soaker thing you got. Marc, I'm with you." John said. Marc looked at John and Alex, then at Ignacia and Amber.

"Actually," Marc said. "Ignacia's with me. John, you're stronger so I want you as the last line of defense for Amber."

"No problem." John said as he took his position next to Amber. Ignacia stood next to Marc and her fists burst into flames. Marc turned to Alex.

"Do you want to stick around or our we ganna have to do this without you?" Marc asked. He had to yell it because the thundering was now directly above them.

"I'm an officer because I live for moments like this." Alex said as he took his jacket off. He looked around for a moment. "I need someone to break that." he said as he pointed at a fire hydrant.

"Too late!" John shouted as the ship ripped through the clouds and slammed into the parking lot.

At that very instant, all the doors flew open and all four soldiers jumped out. Without hesitance, Hercules ran out of the back and started charging toward Alex. Alex began running toward the fire hydrant. Apollo took to the sky. Ignacia turned into a human fireball and flew into the sky like a jet engine. Poseidon ran toward Marc. Marc stood his ground and made his arms turn into solid blocks of ice.

But before Marc could slam his solid fists into Poseidon,

his arms shattered. Poseidon laughed and tackled Marc to the floor. Marc's arms went back to normal as he began to fight with Poseidon,

"So what's your name?" Marc said as he punched Poseidon across the face; the punches were not hurting him as much anymore, and he was hitting harder. Marc knew he was getting stronger with every ability he gained.

"You know my name!" Poseidon said as he pushed Marc off and jumped to his feet. "I'm the god of the sea, Poseidon!"

In the air, Ignacia and Apollo were twisting around each other in a beautiful, aerial dance. Apollo would throw a razor-sharp blast of air and Ignacia would throw a fireball to burn through it. Or Ignacia would fire a blazing projectile and Apollo would snuff it out with a blast of air. Ignacia illuminated the sky in her fiery form. Apollo's silver armor was reflecting a bright orange from Ignacia 's flames.

Alex leaped over the fire hydrant and turned to face his mountainous opponent. Hercules smashed through the hydrant and as soon as the water began to geyser into the air, it froze around Hercules and kept him from moving.

"To bad." Alex said as he pretended to brush his hands off and began running toward Marc.

Then something happened that made everyone stop in his or her tracks. An echoing roar blasted from the center of the emerald, cloud vortex. Then a giant dragon burst through the clouds in a downward path toward Amber. The dragon was massive. It was a dark green color. It was flying with two monstrous arms at its side and tyrannosaurus-like legs. It had spikes at its tail that looked an awful lot like thorns from a vine. The teeth and claws looked like steel. And the head was surrounded by horns that led down its long, snake-like neck.

As the beast got closer to Amber, it began to glow a bright green. And as its snout reached her, it shattered into thousands of little green drops of light that floated in the air for a moment. And just like before, they rushed into Amber through her eyes. John, on the other hand, was thrown back several feet by an invisible force.

The invisible force was really a sonic boom that came from the ship. Marc turned to see what it was. Shriek was standing on top of the ship with one arm aimed at John. Ignacia saw Shriek as well. Shriek's armored gloves were thicker than most and his armor was very bulky by the upper-body; it looked like Shriek would have a hard time moving his head.

Marc took a running start toward Shriek. Poseidon turned away from the dragon spectacle to see Marc with his back turned and decided to take advantage. But as Poseidon created a sharp shard of ice in his hand, a pulse of electricity ran up his legs and stunned him. John shot it through the ground as he stood up.

"What would Marc do without me?" John asked himself as he ran toward Poseidon.

Marc jumped up in an attempt to tackle Shriek off of the ship but Shriek countered with a wall of sonic energy that rattled Marc's entire body to the bone. Marc slammed into the side of the ship as he was forced down by the sonic waves. Marc had a hard time getting up. He could hardly stand. There was a high pitch ringing in his ears that muted the world around him.

What the hell was that? Marc asked himself. Then he felt his entire body go into cramps. He felt this earlier today. He was acquiring a new element; but from who? All his muscles were tightening up. Then a blast of sonic energy nearly flipped the ship over. Shriek was thrown back by the force of the blast and landed on a parked car. Marc let out several blasts as he tried to make his body compensate for the new element. The blasts knocked both Apollo and Ignacia out of the sky. John and Poseidon were separated by one of the blasts. And as the final blast threw so much debris into the air, Alex threw himself around Amber to shield her from it. The blast even freed Hercules from his icy prison.

Several cars had exploded and the alarms of every car within a mile went off. Everyone was on the floor, except for Marc, who was now stumbling to his feet.

"What the hell was that?" John asked as he stood up and dusted himself off.

"I don't know." Marc said as he shook his head. The distant, frantic screams of people in the streets could be heard.

"Check on Shriek!" Apollo yelled to Poseidon, who landed right next to the car that Shriek had landed on. Poseidon had jumped up and pulled Shriek off the roof of the car. Shriek was now standing.

"He seems fine." Poseidon yelled back. But as soon as he did, a fireball slammed into him. Ignacia was walking toward them, still aflame. The fireball threw Poseidon over the car.

"You hit John with a low blow." Ignacia said as she approached Shriek; recalling the sonic wave he hit John with when his back was turned.

Ignacia began to incinerate Shriek with a flame that was blasting out so powerfully that it was pushing Ignacia back. The flame was burning bright blue. The car behind Shriek exploded almost immediately. Poseidon was blow back by the infernal attack.

But the pavement under Shriek melted into a pasty tar, holding him in place. His armor was beginning to melt and the wiring under the bulk of his armor was being fried. Soon, Shriek began to scream. Ignacia stopped the attack to hear what he was saying.

"Stop, for the love of God, stop!" Shriek cried. "Get this crap off of me!" He said as he began tearing at his armor. Ignacia took a step back; she was confused. John ran toward Shriek and helped him rip off Shriek's still-smoldering armor.

The first to come off was the armor around the right arm. When all the metal was stripped from the arm, only bone and little human muscle remained. The arm fell limp to his side. But almost instantly, the muscle began to expand and cover the bone as veins and skin grew throughout the arm.

"Get the rest off of me!" Shriek continued to scream.

"Don't let them!" Apollo said as he shot out toward John, who was finding how to pull off Shriek's chest plate. Apollo grabbed John as he flew by Shriek. John was making his body generate thousands of volts of electricity to make Apollo let him go, but the High General was not letting him go. "I got an upgrade." Apollo said he smashed John into car after car after car.

Ignacia flew after Apollo like a rocket. Marc turned to Poseidon and saw that he was forming the broken shards of ice, from the fire hydrant, into an assortment of jagged spikes. Marc built up a large electric charge in his arms and released it in a bolt of lighting from his palms. The bolt broke through the sub-zero weapons and slammed into Poseidon.

"Are you ok?" Alex asked Amber as he let her go. He stood her up and looked at Hercules, who was preparing to charge at them. Alex quickly looked back at Amber.

"I'm fine. Go get him." Amber said. She began looking at her hands. Alex turned to face Hercules, who was already charging toward them.

"Miss." Alex said to Amber. "You might want to start running." Alex looked to see Marc running toward Poseidon, who was on the floor, and kicking him across the face with an electrically charged foot.

"Marc!" Alex called. Marc turned to look at Alex. "Get prepared to send a bolt right toward the big guy!" Marc nodded.

Alex then broke into thousands of water droplets as Hercules smashed into him and covered the giant machine in water. Marc sent out a massive bolt of lighting that surged through Hercules's body, frying his movement systems and forcing him to fall to the floor in mid-run and slide several feet. Alex reformed on his back on the floor. He was struggling to breath and unable to stand.

"Are you ok?" Amber said as she ran toward Alex.

"I'm fine, but that's the last time I let myself get shocked like that." Alex said as he stood back up.

Hercules was unable to stand back up as sparks flew from his shoulders and back. Marc turned back to Poseidon. Poseidon was struggling to stand back up; he was finished for now. Marc then looked for John and Ignacia. He then saw blue and orange flashed from the sky. When Marc looked up, he saw a fiery figure firing flames at a flying robotic foe that was still carrying John around. Marc ignited his body as well and took to the sky.

[Amber, Alex, take care of the guy that's ripping his armor off.] Marc said as he approached the flying contenders.

"What was that?" Alex said as he stood up.

"Don't worry about it! Come on!" Amber said as she pulled him toward Shriek. Shriek was writhing in pain on the floor, his arm had almost fully regenerated and he was now trying to yank his helmet off.

"Oh my God, I'm hearing voices!" Shriek yelled from the ground.

Amber ran to Shriek and began to pull at his helmet; she was having no luck. Alex pulled her back and simply unlatched the locks around the helmet. The mask then slipped off.

"Ok, how do we get the rest off?" Amber asked as she searched the rest of the mechanical suit.

"With tools." Shriek said as he stumbled to his feet.

"What are you doing?" Alex said as he stood up next to Shriek.

"I'm stopping the fight." Shriek said as he raised one hand into the air. "Cover your ears." He said as he glanced back at Alex and Amber. They covered their ears and looked at each curiously. Then a high-pitched sound that rang in the ears of people that were miles away filled the air. Poseidon began screaming and rolling around on the floor as he tried to cover his ears.

Hercules struggled to pull his hands over his ears. And then Apollo slammed into the floor as he tried to take his helmet off. John landed next to Apollo, but he wasn't moving very much. The noise stopped momentarily.

"Leave!" Shriek yelled at the agonizing, cybernetic beings. "Just leave me alone! I never wanted to be apart of your army!" Shriek then restarted the high pitch noise. The Sentinels could hear the noise, but it wasn't hurting them, to them, it was just loud.

Poseidon and Apollo then struggled to return to the ship as Marc and Ignacia landed. Ignacia couldn't help but throw one more ball of flame at Apollo. The fireball hit Apollo across the back but didn't seem to hurt him as much as the noise.

As the ship began to get airborne, it hovered over to Hercules. As it floated over him, an unseen compartment opened in the rear of the ship and a cable came down to him. Hercules grabbed the cable and it yanked him up. As soon as Hercules was in the ship, the compartment closed and the ship flew away. Shriek then fell to the floor in exhaustion; he had passed out.

"I know where we can take him." Alex said as they crowded around Shriek. "A friend of mine is a mechanic."

"I think we should take him to the hospital." Ignacia said. With worry

"No, first we gatta get the armor off." Marc said.

"I meant him." Ignacia said as she began running to John, who had yet to move.

John was bleeding a lot; he had large gashes all along his face and body. There was glass still sticking into his body from the windshields of the cars in the parking lot.

"Oh God, no." Marc said as he ran toward John. "We're taking John to the hospital first." He said to Alex. Alex just nodded.

CHAPTER 24:

MEETING

"SO I TELL YOU not to lose Shriek, and what do you do?" The man in the suit asked Apollo.

"Sir, we were outnumbered." Apollo said as he stood at attention in front of the suited man's desk. "I wasn't anticipating the intensity of the Fire Anomaly's power."

"Of course you didn't." The suited man said. "Because you never think things through."

"I accept full responsibility, Sir." Apollo said as he bowed his head.

"It makes no difference now." The man said. "I have enough of Isaac's blood to manufacture my remaining generals. I already have a replacement for Shriek." He added as he stood up from behind his desk.

"How did you know I would lose Shriek, Sir?" Apollo asked as he fallowed the man out of the office.

"Because your armor still needs work. And because I suspected that there abilities would continue to grow." The man said as he walked down a cold, windowless hallway. Apollo stopped fallowing the man as he began going the opposite way.

"What are we supposed to do about our armor?" Apollo asked.

"Don't worry." The man said as he turned and began walking toward Apollo. He made Apollo hold his briefcase. He opened it and pulled out a file and closed it, then took the briefcase from Apollo. He gave Apollo the file. "I have it all covered." The man said as he walked away.

Apollo opened the file and began reading through it. Every page had schematics for new armor for all seven Sub-Generals and Apollo, the High General. But as he continued to look through the pages, he saw a suit for someone who was codenamed 'The Morning Star'.

The layout of the suit was surprising to Apollo, mainly because it had much less armor than any of theirs, and also because the 'Morning Star' was labeled as Supreme General. Apollo was under the impression that he would have complete control of the army that was being constructed. The idea of having someone else to take orders from was infuriating.

As Apollo walked into the conference room the next day, he saw that the two remaining Sub-General positions were now filled with people he had never seen before.

"Where did these guys come from?" Apollo asked Aries.

"Well the chick is Athena, she's got biological abilities. And the other dude is Echo, the boss's replacement for

Shriek." Aries said as he referred to the soldier that looked like Shriek, except his armor was not as bulky around the shoulders.

"Where's Morning Star?" Apollo asked as he took a seat next to Aries and Hercules.

"Hell?" Aries said confused. And at that moment, the suited man walked into the room.

All the generals took their seats around a long, rectangular table. The man took his seat at one end of the table. It was odd to see such powerful looking people be so intimidated by such a weak looking man.

"Lady and gentlemen, we are nearing the end off our preparations and nearing the assault." The man said. "We are now in the process of assembling our army of mecha-soldiers."

"Where would we be getting our soldiers from, exactly?" Athena asked.

"The world's militaries lose soldiers everyday, actually losing a few won't raise any eyebrows in time. We also take John Does from morgues." The man said.

"How many soldiers do we have so far?" Apollo asked. The man began looking through several papers that were in front of him.

"There will be over four hundred by the end of the day." The man said as he looked at his watch. "Add that to the soldiers from last week and we have over a thousand." He added.

"Just over a thousand?" Apollo asked in skepticism. "That's our army?"

"These soldiers have already been equipped with the new armor I've designed." The man said, ignoring what Apollo just said, a screed turned on behind him. I showed a blueprint of these mecha-soldiers. "They will have one visor across the eyes that allows for x-ray, thermal, and magnified vision." The man said as he described the soldiers. "They will have a right arm that converts into an arm canon that fires a range of weapons from high caliber bullets, to flame retardant foam." He continued. Parts of the blueprint on screen began to glow as he described them. "This new armor is more durable to the attacks of these Anomalies."

"So we'll be going up against them again?" Hercules asked.

"I would really love to go up against them again." Aries said with a laugh.

"I have a few bones to pick with them." Poseidon said.

"Calm down." The man said with a smile on his face. "You will all have your chances to go up against them later."

"What's the plan now, Sir?" Athena asked.

"All in due time." The man said, still smiling. "First I want to equip you all with the new armor. This way, you'll all be able to take down our foes a lot easier." Everyone cheered and began to clap.

CHAPTER 25:

JUST WAITING

AS PEOPLE GOT OFF the elevator, Ignacia noticed that Alex and Marc were among them. A third man wearing sunglasses was fallowing them. The third man didn't seem much older than Alex, who was twenty-five. The man had longer hair that reached just a little past his shoulders. He seemed skinny and malnourished.

"How's he doing?" Marc asked Ignacia, as he walked by her.

"The doctor said he would be fine." Ignacia said as she stood up. "We're just waiting for you guys. He's awake already."

"The doctor said John is doing better than anyone else

he's seen with less severe injuries." Amber commented.

"Is this. . ." Ignacia started to say to the man with sunglasses. The man looked to be lost as he didn't look at anyone directly.

"I'm Isaac." The man said as he held one hand out. Ignacia shook his hand. "I used to be Shriek."

"So let's get in there and see if he's awake." Alex said as he opened the door to the room that John was being held in. As everyone walked into the room, John was just watching TV. He smiled as soon as he realized who it was that was walking into the room.

"What took you so long?" John said as he sat himself up in his hospital bed. "No offense, Alex, but British TV sucks." As John saw Isaac enter the room behind Ignacia he couldn't help but say. "Is this. . ."

"I'm Isaac." Isaac said again as he walked over to John to shake his hand. John hesitated for a second before shaking Isaac's hand.

"Sorry about that." John said. "It's just that the last time we met, you blasted me in the back."

"Don't sweat it, I would be a little iffy too." Isaac said as he sat down. He still didn't look at anyone directly.

"Hey." John said. "You're that guy that got kidnapped, aren't you?" He asked. "Your dad owns Chimer-Tech Industries."

"Yes, that would be me." Isaac said.

"So how are you feeling Johnny?" Amber asked.

"I'll be fine. Marc, what's the plan?" John responded as he turned the TV off and tried to sit up straight.

"Well as soon as we get out of here, we should try to see if we can find a nice secluded place to work on our fighting." Marc said.

"Sounds like a plan." John said, as he looked Isaac out of the corner of his eyes. Isaac didn't seem to notice John's eyes.

"So John," Isaac said. "Why so nervous?" he asked with a smile. John looked at him with interest.

"What makes you think I'm nervous?" John asked curiously. He wondered how Isaac knew he was nervous.

"Your heart is beating faster." Isaac said.

"Well you haven't taken your glasses off since you walked in here." John said as he signaled to Marc to hand him his clothes.

"Well we tried to take everything out of my body that was mechanical." Isaac said as he reached for his glasses. "And my eyes had been replaced." Isaac took the glasses off and revealed that he had no eyes. "And when we took the implants out, my eyes didn't grow back." he said grimly as Marc handed John a bag that was sitting on a chair.

"That sucks, dude." John said. "So why don't you look like your dad?" he asked, noticing that Isaac's skin was darker than his famous father's.

"My mom." Isaac answered. "She was Indian and my dad is Australian. Does that answer your question?"

"Not really." John said. "I've seen your dad talk, like, a hundred times on TV since you were supposedly kidnapped and he doesn't haven't an accent."

"I know." Isaac said. "He hides it well." Everyone in the room was quiet for a moment.

"Well if you can all kindly get out, I'm about to change into my civvies." John said as began getting out of bed.

"I'll wait here." Ignacia said as she sat down in the chair

outside the of John's room.

"Ok," Marc said. "We'll be in the parking lot." He added as they began to walk into the elevator.

A few moments later, John walked out of the room and toward Ignacia. She was reading a magazine, or at least pretending to. When she looks up at John, she closed the magazine and stood up.

"Are you ready to get out of here?" Ignacia asked as she put her hands in her pockets.

"Yeah." John said with a smile on his face. "So were you worried about me?" He asked as they began to walk to the elevator.

"Not so much." Ignacia joked. "I was actually enjoying the quiet." As they walked into an elevator, everyone else got out. They were left alone in the elevator.

"So do we have a place to practice our fighting yet?" John asked. Ignacia ignored his question.

"You know you never answered my question." Ignacia said as she looked down at her feet.

"And what question would that be?" John asked as he pushed the button that would take them to the first floor.

"Why don't you just admit that you like me?" Ignacia asked. As she asked this question, the doors closed.

John stayed quiet for a while. He looked at Ignacia and noticed that she was staring at him, and not looking away. He just stared back at her, thinking of an answer. Then, before John could think of anything to say, he had dropped his bag and started kissing her. She didn't stop him.

CHAPTER 26:

PREPPING

"OK, SO I KNOW of a perfect place we can use for practice." Alex said on the bus ride to his house.

The six of them were all in the back of the second deck of a double-decker bus. John and Ignacia were in the very back row of seats, still kissing. Amber had a seat all to herself; she had her feet up. Marc was sitting in front of Amber as he looked through his bag for his MP3 player.

"Where would that be?" Isaac asked as he pressed one hand against a window.

"There is a large field outside of town." Alex said, "If we can get a few trees around a large area of it. . ."

"That sounds like a plan." Marc said. "But I think we

should get some shut-eye first. It is seven o'clock." John pulled away from Ignacia for a moment.

"And why do we need to sleep again?" John asked. "It's not like we have to anymore." John pointed out.

John had raised a good point. Ever since their abilities awoke in them, they no longer needed to sleep, eat, drink, or even rest at all when they perform normal human activities. Marc thought about this for a while. Then he came to a decision about what to do.

"We'll need lighting." Marc said as he began pulling things out of his bag, still looking for his MP3 player.

"We?" Isaac said with a smile on his face.

"Don't worry about that." Alex said. "I have lights and generators at my house. I have it all covered."

"Why are you so prepared?" John asked Alex. " You seem to have so a lot of resources. You had a private mechanic to work on Isaac, your house is big enough for all of us, and now you have enough equipment to host an outdoor soccer game at night. Why do you have these things?"

"Because I like to play *futbol* at night." Alex replied sarcastically.

"Can you get all that out there by tonight?' Marc asked Alex.

"I'll have to barrow my neighbors truck, but yes." Alex said assertively.

"Well let's get to it." Marc said.

Almost an hour later, a blue truck pulls to the side of a lone road, just outside of London. A black car pulled up behind it. Alex was driving the truck; Marc and Isaac were with him. Everyone else was in the car behind them. As everyone began to pile out of the car, Marc and Alex began unloading the lights and generators.

"How far out are we going?" Isaac asked as he walked over to Marc.

"About a kilometer should do it." Alex said. Marc and Isaac just stared at him; a look of confusion on both their faces. "You both know how far a kilometer is, right?" Alex asked as he saw their faces. "I'll just say when to stop walking, ok?'

"That would be nice." Marc said.

As they all walked out into the middle of the field, Alex looked back to see how far the road was. At one point he stopped walking and stared back at the road and began to put down the equipment he was carrying.

"I think the wall of trees should start here." Alex said.

"Wow," John said as he caught up with them. "We're about a kilometer out." Marc just stared at John for moment.

"Let's start setting up." Marc said. "Amber, you think you can set up the wall by yourself?" he asked.

"Yeah, I got it." She said as a tree sprang up out of the ground right in front of her. Within moments, the tree was over twenty feet tall.

Within a few minutes, the barrier of trees was half done, and the lights were all set up. Marc began helping Amber set the trees up.

"Ok, it looks like we're all done." Marc said as he set up the last tree. "What time is it?" he asked.

"It's almost four." John said as he repositioned a light.

The lights were set up in a large square that was over thirty feet in length. The arena they had set up was well lit, but too small for all of them to spar at once.

"Ok, we'll have to go two at a time." Marc said. "So who's first on the chopping block?" he asked.

"I'll go." John said as he began stretching his shoulder and legs "I wanna see how much I rock." He joked.

"Me too." Isaac added with a laugh. "Better yet. Let's see if you can beat a blind man."

"Ok, a couple ground rules. When one says stop, you stop. . . That's it." Marc said. "Oh and not to flashy." He added quickly.

CHAPTER 27:

SPARRING

"SO TO RECAP," MARC said. "In the fight between John and Isaac, Isaac won. And in the fight between Amber and Alex, Amber won."

"It's just you and me." Ignacia said to Marc. "So stop stalling and let's get to it already."

The sun was beginning to rise over the trees. Alex had turned off the lights after his fight with Amber. Marc took his position near the center of the arena. Ignacia did the same; she got into a right-handed boxing position. Marc just put his fists up in front of his face.

"I'm not going easy on you." Marc said.

"I'm not either." Ignacia said.

Marc threw a sonic blast from his fist as he threw a punch. Ignacia jumped to one side and launched a giant flame through the sonic blast. Marc then blocked the flame with a wall of water that that froze into an ice-shield. Ignacia shot a larger, continues flame at the shield. Marc and the shield disappeared into the flame. Ignacia stopped the blast and saw Marc was no longer there. She quickly looked around and didn't see him. Water then began to mound up behind her. It formed into Marc. Marc then hit her from behind with a ball of water. Ignacia flew forward several feet but anchored her feet and fist into the ground and turned around quickly. As she turned, she flung her hand into the air and launched a fireball toward Marc. Marc had jumped to his left but instead of passing by him, the fireball exploded.

Marc was thrown several feet by the explosion. As he slammed into the floor, Marc rolled, and quickly hopped back onto his feet. He almost immediately started throwing sonic blasts from his hands as he started running toward Ignacia. Ignacia was running toward Marc as well; she launched fireballs back at him. The two of them were both taking sidesteps as they dodged each other's attacks. As they got closer and closer to colliding with each other, their attacks intensified to larger sonic blasts and larger fireballs. Finally, they were just inches from each other and they both threw haymaker punches toward each other; Ignacia's fist was consumed in flames, Marc's fist was surging with electrical energy. Both fists smashed into one another; Marc was sent flying back as an explosion erupted from Ignacia's fist, Ignacia dropped to the floor as her muscles locked up from the voltage that was coursing through her body.

Marc slammed into a tree and fell to the floor. As he stood up, a root from the tree shot out of the ground, toward Ignacia. Ignacia was just getting to her feet when the root starting to wrap around her body; it lifted her into the air. Ignacia tried to burn off the root by making herself burst into flame. But the root just got thicker and thicker as it tightened around her.

"Stop!" Ignacia yelled as she slapped her free hand against the outside of the root. The root then gently put her down as it loosened its grip around her. She started taking in deep breaths as she lay back in the grass. Marc walked over to her to help her to her feet.

"That was fun." Marc said as he helped Ignacia stand up. She laughed as she patted herself down.

"I really think it's unfair that you have more than one element." Ignacia said. She turned and saw John walking toward her.

Marc and John gave each other a high five as they past one another. John continued to Ignacia and gave her a hug. Marc was receiving praises by the other sentinels.

"That was fun." John said. "You almost had him, kinda, in a way. Not really though."

"Almost isn't good enough." Ignacia said. "I need to work on controlling my powers."

"Why do you say that?" John asked as they started walking toward the group. "I think you did pretty well"

"My boxing instructor told me the same thing. 'Te tienes que controlar el humor.'" Ignacia said as she impersonated an elderly Mexican man.

"You have to control your mood?" John said as he tried to translate her words.

CHAPTER 28:

SCORING HIGH

APOLLO ENTERED THE COLD, steel hallway; the Sub-Generals were all standing along the wall, talking amongst themselves.

"What were your scores?" Apollo asked. "Sound off as I pass you." He added as he walked down the hall toward a reinforced, circular door.

"Forty-two over one hundred." Coronus said.

"Nine-teen over one hundred." Echo said.

"Twenty over one hundred." Athena said.

"Thirty-six over one hundred." Aries said.

"Twenty-four over one hundred." Poseidon said.

"Sixty-nine over one hundred." Hercules said.

"Twenty-nine over one hundred." Zeus said.

"You're all pitiful." Apollo said as he stood in front of the circular door. "I'll show you how a High General scores on his performance test."

The circular door opened and Apollo stepped into the small chamber. The chamber was so small it was hard to believe that Hercules could fit in there. Then a wall of the chamber dropped and became a ramp that led to a grand tunnel that twisted and turned. Apollo didn't run into the tunnel, he shot into it. As he flew through the tunnel, dummies began popping out from behind barriers. Machine guns were popping out of the walls and firing at Apollo.

Apollo did not stop flying forward. He flung his hands forward and launched blade-like blasts of wind that shot through the tough target dummies. He moved swiftly through the air as he dodged the bullets of the machine guns. Eventually, rockets were fired at him. He sliced the rockets in half with his aero-abilities and flew through the fiery explosion without harm.

Once in a while, Apollo was hit by a straight bullet and failed to land a fatal injury on the target dummies, but he paid those no attention. He was concerned with the walls that were closing ahead of him too much to take time for precision. At the very end of the long tunnel, there was a target dummy that was firing rockets and machine guns at him. Apollo launched several blasts of wind at it, but this one was built to be very sturdy. In the end, Apollo focused a large amount of his energy into one powerful blast of wind. The blast ripped the dummy from the floor and smashed it through the door.

Apollo walked out of the tunnel through a door on the other side of the hallway that the other generals were waiting in. There was a small screen on the right of the door. It was tabulating his score. After a few short seconds, it displayed his score. It read 'eighty-nine over one hundred'. Apollo was impressed with himself. He proudly walked over to the other generals. They, for some reason, seemed unimpressed; if anything, they were looking at the circular door, which was closing as Apollo approached them.

"Who just stepped in?" Apollo asked as he scanned the generals to see who was missing from the group.

"My secret weapon." The man in the suit said as he entered the hallways from the flight of steps behind Apollo.

"Is that Morning Star?' Apollo asked.

"No," the man responded. "This one is no general. He is simply a weapon. He is not fused with any elemental forces, so I could replace much of his body with machine. This allows him to carry heavier weaponry, tougher armor, and I almost comply switched out his brain for one of my more obedient ones. He is my machine of war."

"What's his name?" Hercules asked.

"I call him Hates." The man said.

Loud booms could be heard from the iron walls behind them. This was impossible since there was at least fourteen inches of metal that made up those walls.

"What course is he taking?" Apollo asked as the crashes continued.

"He is taking your course, Sir." Echo said with hesitance.

"Lets see if he can do any better than I did." Apollo said sarcastically.

Apollo regretted his last statement as the door opened and a mecha-soldier, the size of Hercules, walked out.

Hates did not stop there. He continued to walk toward the stairs and out of the hallway. The score was finally tabulated shortly after Hates left. The score read 'ninety-four over one hundred'.

"What do you know, Jake," The man smiled. "A mindless machine outdid you by five points." The man said as he walked away.

"You still scored very high, Sir." Poseidon said. "It's still something to be proud of. You did way better than I did."

"Shut up!" Apollo barked. He began to walk up the stairs. Apollo would not take this lying down.

CHAPTER 29:

READY TO RUMBLE

"Now I've never done this before, but the First said it could be done." Marc said as he and the sentinels sat in a circle on Alex's living room floor. "Just, everyone, think about your element and think about how you feel as you use it." Marc continued.

All their eyes began to glow; John's eyes were glowing bright, neon blue; Ignacia's eyes were glowing orange-red; Amber's eyes were glowing bright green; Alex's eyes were glowing dark blue; Isaac's eyes obviously did not glow, but silent waves were pulsating from behind the sunglasses; And Marc's eyes were alternating from neon blue, to dark blue, to green, to orange-red, to plain white, and to dark green.

"Now concentrate those feelings on me." Marc said.

Then, for some reason, the sun began to set; at noon, the sun was set. Then a man, who looked a lot like Marc, appeared before them, in the middle of the circle.

"Who are you?" Amber asked.

"I am the First." He answered. "Take the glasses off." He said as he turned to Isaac.

Isaac took his sunglasses off. His eyes had returned to him. They were glowing white. Isaac began to look around the room, and at his own body.

"How is this possible?" Isaac asked.

"We are in Marc's mind." The First said. "Anything is possible in the human mind." The First walked over to Marc. "You guys can stand now." He said as he approached Marc.

Everyone stood up and continued to stare at the First. They didn't seem to understand who he was. Even after the countless times Marc had explained to them about the warrior in his mind, they still did not expect to see him.

"Why do you look so much like Marc?" John asked.

"It's easier for me to assume the form of someone you all know." The First said. "Are you guys hungry?"

As they all sat down at the kitchen table, the First was beginning to look through Alex's refrigerator. All, except for Marc, were still staring at him in awe.

"So what's the plan, Marc?" The First asked as he looked through the articles of food in the fridge.

"Well that's why we came to you." Marc said as he leaned back in his chair.

"Well do you know who the bad guys are yet?" The First asked as he sniffed something that was wrapped in foil.

"Well we don't really know who the bad guys are yet." John said finally as he scratched his head.

"I do." Isaac said. Everyone turned to look him, except for the First. "I know them al by name."

"You're Isaac, right?' The First asked.

"Yeah," Isaac responded.

"You used to be a bad guy, right?" The First asked.

"Yes." Isaac continued.

"And no one has thought to ask you anything, right?" The First said laughing. Everyone then stared at Marc, except John.

"It just slipped our minds." John said. He glanced at Marc for a second; as if to say 'I just saved you from getting blamed'. Everyone then looked at Isaac.

"Enlighten us." The First said as he sat down in a chair.

"Well," Isaac started. "My father is the owner of Chimer-Tech. A few years ago, he was researching a way to splice specific animal genes to human genes, to make people live longer, fight harder, and consume less."

"Why was he researching that?" Amber asked.

"He figured he could get a military contract I guess. Who wouldn't want some super soldiers?" Isaac said. "He was really stressed. Anything would set him off. I got into an argument with him one day. It got really bad. I remember I yelled at him, and. . ." Isaac stopped talking for a moment. There were tears in his eyes. "There was this blast. It collapsed the roof of our house. When I woke up, I was in the hospital. It had been a week since the accident. My dad told me that my mom had died in the collapse." Marc looked at Amber; her eyes were tearing up as well.

"Where did the blast come from?" Ignacia asked.

"It was a sonic boom that I screamed out. I don't know how it happened." Isaac continued. "Then my dad just seemed different. He wasn't stressed from work anymore. He seemed happier for some reason. Then he asked if he could study me, like I wasn't even his son anymore. I told him no. But he insisted. It was like that for days. Finally, I was about to move out, but some people had broken into our home. They were after me and not my dad. He just let them take me." Isaac was on the verge of crying. "My dad had hired them to take me to his private lab. And there, he started to probe me, suck out buckets of blood at a time, and doing things that I can only describe as medical torture. One day he just plugged a computer into my brain and made me into that monster." Isaac was now crying. There were tears running down the side of his face. "My own father. How can he do that to me?" The First walked over to Isaac. He leaned down to look Isaac in the eyes.

"Isaac," The First said. "Can you remember where this lab is?" he asked.

"He's not at the old lab." Isaac said as he dried his tears. "He shut it down and we moved to his new facility when the investigation over my kidnapping started."

"Where is it?" Marc asked.

"It's in Alaska." Isaac said. "Just north of Dry Lake."

"Can we get there on foot?" Marc asked.

"Yeah." Isaac responded after thinking for a few seconds. "There is a foot trail that goes right by there."

"Well it looks like you guys have a destination." The First said. At that moment, they all snapped out of their trance.

They were all still on the living room floor in a circle.

Everyone, except for Marc, was looking around confused for moment. He stood up and walked over to the window. He was stretching his back and cracking his knuckles. John walked over to Marc.

"What do we do now?" John asked.

"Why are you asking me?' Marc asked confused.

"Well you're the leader here." John explained as he turned to look out the window.

"And who said I was the leader?" Marc said. "I never said I wanted to be the leader. I'm a DJ for Christ sake."

"Watch your mouth," John said. "And you weren't a DJ. But you are the strongest one out of all of us."

"How do you figure?" Marc asked. He turned to look around the house; everyone was doing different things. Amber was sitting with Isaac, trying to calm him down. Alex and Ignacia were in the kitchen; Ignacia was looking through the fridge and Alex was talking to someone over the phone.

"You kicked Nacha's ass the other night, for one thing." John said as he continued to look out the window. "And Nacha kicks a lot of ass." He added with a smile.

"What is with you and her anyway?" Marc asked in an attempt to change the subject.

"She wants my body." John said jokingly.

"Don't mess this up." Marc warned. "If you mess things up with her, and something happens. . ." he was interrupted by John.

"And there is that leader I was talking about." John pointed out. Marc didn't want to admit it, but John was right.

"Well we have to stop these attacks." Marc said. "It

won't be long till they find us here. The news about the dragon at the hotel will spread."

"Well do you want to get down there and take out some baddies?" John asked.

"I don't want to risk their lives." Marc said as he faced the window again.

"Marc," John said. "I'm coming with you, ok? And noting is going to happen to us. We are invincible!" he said sternly.

"So it's decided." Marc said as he raised his voice for everyone to here. "We are assaulting the bad guys for once, at their base. Anyone who doesn't want to join in, speak now."

No one said a thing.

CHAPTER 30:

BORROW, ALASKA

"I WAS EXPECTING MORE snow than this?" Ignacia sarcastically said as they stepped into a diner.

"I know how you feel." John said as he took off a large sweater. "I didn't think I would freeze just walking from the airport."

The sentinels sat at two separate tables and began looking through the menus. Amber and Marc were sitting with Isaac, and John and Ignacia were sitting with Alex on the other side of the diner. They did not want to look like a large group in case someone would see them and report their location. Amber had begun reading the menu to Isaac.

"Hold on, Amber." Marc said. "Isaac, how are we ganna get to Dry Lake? I saw a map of Alaska at the airport and we are pretty far from Dry Lake."

"I probably should have been more specific." Isaac explained. "The main facility is *under* Dry Lake. The reason I wanted to come to Borrow is because there is a zoom-tube here."

"Zoom-tube?" Amber asked.

"I'll show you when we find it." Isaac said.

While this conversation was going on at one end of the diner, John, Ignacia and Alex were having an entirely different conversation. Ever since John met Alex, he has had questions about Alex's resources. Alex just seemed to have everything covered: the location for training, lighting, a place for all of them to stay, and he even had the means to get to Alaska.

"So how do you have all this cash and crap at your huge house?" John asked as he looked through the menu.

"Excuse me?" Alex said s he put his menu down.

"John wants to know why you are so fortunate to be prepared to house and fund us." Ignacia elaborated.

"Well that's simple." Alex said. "My dad."

"What about your dad?" John asked.

"He had friends in positions of power." Alex said. "He would receive money from them and process it for usage."

"Your dad laundered money for gangsters?" John asked.

"That would be a simpler way to say it, but yes." Alex said. "He was also a cop." Alex said with disappointment.

"What happen to your dad?" Ignacia asked.

"He had a large order come in for a very powerful business associate." Alex said. "Someone working with my dad took the cash and ran. My dad tried to explain to these people what had happened, they didn't believe him. My dad got stuck with the blame. And they made him disappear."

"When did all this happen?" John asked.

"When I was nineteen." Alex said. "I decided to join the force almost immediately after that. A few years ago, I found out who ran with the money. Apparently he was still in the game." Alex made quotation marks in the air with his fingers. "His name is Charlie Turner. I was working on getting him myself. A few months ago, I found him. He had just made a deal with someone. I caught him red handed. I chased him to a warehouse and, there was this accident. A bullet hit a fuse box, and it had been raining. Everything was wet. I almost died. Turner was not seen after that."

"That sucks." John exclaimed. "You had your shot for vengeance and you lost him." Alex just glanced at John from his menu.

"I'm sure that's what he wants to hear, John." Ignacia said, pointing out John's insensitivity.

"But hey," John continued. "You may bump into him again. You never know, you know?"

"I hope so." Alex said as he saw the waitress approach them.

[Guys, we'll be leaving soon.] Marc said with mental network he had just established with his friends. [So eat up and get ready.]

[I can't eat when I'm being rushed.] John said.

"Oh shut up." Ignacia said with a smile.

CHAPTER 31:

UNDERGROUND

"SO WHAT ARE WE looking for exactly?" Marc asked as they all followed Isaac.

"We're looking for a warehouse that looks like it's closed." Isaac explained. "It should be around here somewhere."

"I see a warehouse just up the street." John said. "And it looks closed."

"Does it have a sign or something?" Isaac asked.

"Yeah, it says 'Piping and carting'. Not very catchy." John joked.

"But that's where we are headed." Isaac said. "This is here just in case if one of the thunder-bringers crash landed just outside of base."

"Thunder-bringers?" Marc asked.

"The ships we cruised around in." Isaac explained. "My dad didn't know what else to call them."

They all walked behind the warehouse. Marc picked up a chip of cement and threw it through a window. He reached his arm in and unlocked the window. He opened it and one by one, they climbed in through the window. The window led to an office. The picture frames had no pictures in them. The clock on the wall was not ticking. And when they walked out of the office, into the main floor, everything looked abandoned.

"So what are we looking for now?" Amber asked. She sounded nervous. Marc could tell she didn't want to be there; in fact, everyone could tell.

"Anyone who doesn't want to continue has to bail out now." John said. In reality, he was directing the statement to Amber.

"After what happened to Craig, I'm not bailing out now." Amber said. "I want to get that golden one to myself."

They proceeded to walk behind Isaac. Ignacia stopped walking and waited for Amber to catch up to her. As Amber passed her by, she grabbed her by the arm and pulled her aside.

"Ok listen," Ignacia began. "If we get into a big fight down there, and you run out on us, I will hunt you down and torch you myself."

"What is wrong with you?" Amber asked. "Since I met you you've seemed to have had a problem with me. Why is that?"

"Are you kidding me?" Ignacia asked sarcastically. "I

know people like you. Since birth, you have had everything handed to you, because of your parents. And in situations like this, I bet that the only thing you would think about is yourself." Ignacia was beginning to raise her voice. The rest of the group had continued looking through the warehouse.

"You think I'm a rich-girl stereotype?" Amber asked. She seemed offended. "Let me tell you something, chica! I went to the same public schools you undoubtedly went to. I met all the same people. I learned all the same things. And I even learned the same morals." Amber was now raising her voice. "The only difference between me and you is that I actually wanted to help people and I actually can. What have you been doing with your life? Hitting other people because a guy with a whistle told you so?"

Ignacia still looked mad, only now she wasn't saying anything. She was embarrassed that she had made such a bold accusation toward someone she didn't even know. But her doggedness would never let her admit her mistake.

"Uh, girls," John said from a doorway on the far side of the warehouse. "If you're done bickering, we found the zoom-tube. But maybe we can get some mud wrestling later."

As Amber followed Ignacia through the doorway, she looked at the doorstep. It looked like the entrance to an elevator. The small room they entered had glass walls. One glass wall just faced a regular wall. It seemed a bit redundant. There were several large chairs with seatbelts attached to them. All the chairs in the room were facing either the door or the glass wall that was placed over the regular wall.

"Stay away from the door." Isaac warned as he strapped into a chair. Everyone took a hint from Isaac's actions and did the same.

"What now?" John said after a brief silence.

"R.T.B!" Isaac shouted. And as soon as he said that, the entire room dropped twenty feet below ground. The glass wall was no longer facing another wall; instead it was facing and endless tunnel that was dimly lit. The room then slowly began moving through the tunnel. It began to pick up speed gradually. Finally, the room was traveling so quickly that everything outside the glass walls was just a blur. Even though the room was moving so quickly, everything in the room was stable.

"It'll be a short trip." Isaac said. "So if you have any last minute planning, say it now."

"We'll need to stick to the shadows." Marc said. "Avoid confrontation at all times. There is a good chance that the last four sentinels are still in there somewhere. They are our top priority." Everyone nodded as the room began to slow down. It completely stopped and began to descend again.

"How far down is this lab?" John asked.

"Very." Isaac said.

"How big is the lab?" Marc asked.

"Very." Isaac said. The room had stopped. Everyone faced the door.

"Well, let's get out there." Marc said.

CHAPTER 32:

UNKNOWING PRISONERS

"So why are we in lockdown?" Said a young man with a Russian accent.

He was sitting in a room with three other people; on the other side of the room were two girls, identical twins, reading; and in the back of the room, by a TV, was another young man playing a loud arcade game.

"Well apparently there was a break in." The second young man said with a German accent. He leaned back in his seat as he beat the level he was currently playing.

"Did anyone hear when we are getting out of here?" one of the twins said with a Latin accent.

"Jesus, Blanca?" the other twin said with the same accent. "You've been asking that for weeks now. I thought you'd be used to this place by now."

"Sorry, Carla." Blanca said as she began reading again. "I just want to see the sun again before I die." She added sarcastically.

"Can you believe these two, Tobias?" The Russian man said to the German. "They fight more than a married couple."

The noise in the room was quickly silenced as loud bangs could be heard behind the securely locked door that looked like it was once part of a bank vault. Gunshots could be heard. It sounded like automatic rifles were being used. Everyone in the room was just staring at the door.

"Greg, check the door." Blanca said to the Russian man from the couch. She and her sister were both nervous.

As Greg stood up, his skin seemed to turn to stone. He walked over to the door and began to unlock it. As the door began to open, the gunfire and booms stopped. The door slowly swung open. A short Mexican girl stood before them; her skin was smoking, she was hyperventilating, her hands were holding fireballs.

"Hi, I am Ignacia Castillo." She said.

"And I'm her young stallion." John said as he poked his head from behind the door. "And we will be saving you this evening."

"What do you mean by saving us?" Carla asked as she, her sister, Greg, and Tobias followed John and Ignacia though the cold, metallic hallways. The bodies of unconscious guards littered the floor.

"Let me ask you guys something." John said. "Have you guys had any weird feeling lately? Like you've been doing things that you could never have done before." John then looked back at Greg, who was still in his rocky form. "Never mind."

"Well the guy who brought you here has been creating robotic soldiers with your abilities." Ignacia said. "And they have been trying to kill us."

"Why is Abe trying to kill you?" Carla asked. "He seems so nice."

"The Devil's greatest accomplishment was convincing the word he didn't exist." John said as he peeked around a corner.

"Abe is trying to kill us because we won't join him." Ignacia said. "Unlike you guys, we don't trust people who threaten the lives of innocent people."

"He said he just wanted to study us." Tobias said. "Abraham didn't say anything about soldiers."

"Nacha, I have a question." John said to Ignacia. "If we were causing a distraction for Marc and the others to find these lovely people, and we found them, where are Marc and the others headed?"

"Nacha Castillo?" Carla asked. "I am pretty sure that I know that name from somewhere."

"No you don't." Ignacia said immediately.

"Hey, big guy." John said to the muscular Russian man. "What is in the far side of the facility?"

"We don't know." Greg said. "We were only allowed access to the dormitories and rec. rooms."

"Who know what they're running into over there." Ignacia said. "But I hope they're doing ok."

"We have to get over there!" John said.

CHAPTER 33:

THE STORM

JOHN RAN TOWARD SEVERAL guards. But before any guard could fire a single shot from their automatic rifles, John shot out what appeared to be net made of electricity. The net ran along the circular hallway and smashed into the guards that blocked the hallway. The guards seized up and fell to the floor in a paralyzed state. John did not stop running; he leaped over the limp bodies as they fell. Ignacia and the others followed close behind.

"How did he get so skilled?" Tobias asked.

"He came in contact with the Chimera." Ignacia said as she ran along the hallway.

"What's that?" Blanca asked.

"A man named Marc." Ignacia said as she saw John

approached a large circular door.

John looked around to find a way to open the door. It didn't seem to have a way to open from the side he was currently on. Loud explosions could be heard on the other side of the door.

"Move!" Greg said as his rocky skin turned to a much denser material. He slammed his shoulder into the door several times. The door then crashed open.

As the door crashed open, John saw that it lead to a grand hall that appeared to be the center of the whole compound. The hall looked to be designed for looks. It was a tall room that reached up to eight stories. There were tall pillars that were made of marble. The round room had armed guards at every floor. Each one was firing into the center of the bottom level.

Marc and the others were in the middle of the hall; behind a small ice-wall. Gaps opened in the wall of ice for moments at a time for Marc and Isaac to launch sonic blasts through. Amber was launching large, slim seeds that stabbed into the wall, sprouting vines that ensnared guards. The seeds were flying out so quickly that it was hard to see where they were coming from; she was just flicking them like cards from her hand. The vines would only hold the guards for as long as it took for them to cut themselves out.

As John ran into the room, a rocket was launched from an upper level. The rocket exploded just in front of John, launching him against the wall by the door he had just ran in through. He was knocked out cold.

Ignacia was about to run in after him but Greg held her back. He had turned his skin to marble and ran into the hall. Bullets were just bouncing off his skin. He aimed his hands at a pillar. The pillar shot several chunks of itself at any guards that were standing by it on all levels. He did the same with every other pillar. As soon as the firing subsided to just a few shots, Ignacia ran out and pulled John into the hallway. Marc and the others saw their opening. They ran toward the hallway to join the newly freed prisoners.

"How's John?" Marc asked as he looked down at his friend, who was down for the count.

"His arm is broken and both his shoulders seem dislocated. But I think he'll be fine." Ignacia said as she rested John's head on her lap.

John's bones could be heard crunching back into place. A cut over his brow had stopped bleeding already. His eyes were beginning to open.

"Damn!" Marc said. "You just took a big hit."

"Is the other guy ok?" John joked as he looked up at Ignacia.

"So is this everybody?" Marc asked as he helped John to his feet.

"Yeah." John said as he looked back at the new group members. "The big guy is Greg, tall and skinny over there is Tobias, and the dream team is Blanca and Carla." John said as he pointed each one out. When he looked to face Marc again, he noticed his friend was holding his sides and breathing harder and harder.

"Marc, are you ok?" Amber asked as she put one hand on his back. "Did you get hit?"

"Get him out of the hallway!" John said as he grabbed Marc and dragged him back into the hall. "Last three elements at once." John said to Marc as guards began aiming their guns at them. "Can you handle it?"

"I hope so." Marc said as he fell to his knees. He was gritting his teeth and breathing very hard.

"You better," John said. "Because I'm not leaving your side." John knelt down in front of Marc and put his hands on Marc's shoulders.

Just before any guard could get a shot off, wind began to pick up in a circular movement. The spiraling wind was making guards fall to the floor and even slide several feet. The wind grew to hurricane status. John continued to hold on to Marc, who was on the edge of yelling. No guard was able to stand still, let alone aim their weapon.

The wind then stopped and the pillars began to crack. Small shards of each pillar were shooting out like shotgun shells. These jagged pebbles were pelting guards, and some were being killed; John's back and arms became riddled with these jagged shards as well. But still, John held his ground. Marc let out cries of pain. The entire hall was on the verge of collapsing as it began to shake.

Suddenly, everything stopped shaking. Then all the light in the room was sucked into Marc. He was the only visible thing in the hall, which was completely black. Then beams of light shot out of Marc in every direction as he screamed in agony. The beams were pulsating several different colors and scorched anything they touched. Any guard that was still alive was killed after a beam of light sliced through him. The beams had no affect on John, as his element is a bright, hot light. Then the hall went back to normal.

The hall was silent as the other sentinels walked in slowly. All the guards were either dead or unconscious. The hall looked like the remains of a battlefield. Ignacia approached John and Marc. John stood upright and walked to Ignacia. She began picking the shards of marble out of John's back.

"Are you ok, Marc?" John asked. Marc was standing up slowly. He would not stop looking at his hands. Marc looked like he was in awe.

"I can feel them." Marc whispered out loud.

"Feel what?" Amber asked.

"The elements." Marc said. "All of them. I can feel the sun, the moon, the ocean, and the sky, the Earth. I can feel it all." Marc closed his fists. "And it feels good."

"Well let's get out of here already." John said. "I kinda don't like standing around while people with guns are looking for us."

"We can't yet." Marc said as he turned to face them. "We need to find the way they were tracking us and destroy it." Marc turned to look at the new sentinels. "Do you guys know where it might be?" he asked.

"The broadcast center." Tobias said. "It's the only part of the compound that is viewable from the surface."

"Where do we go from here?" Marc asked. He was still looking at his hands. He felt different in almost every single way.

"It is directly over this hall." Blanca said. "It is how they brought us in. The docking bay is accessible from there as well."

"Do you remember how to get up there?" John asked as he picked the last of the marble out of his back.

"I do." Carla said. "I have a good memory." She added, a bit conceitedly.

"You lead the way." Marc said.

CHAPTER 34:

CLASH

As THE GROUP RAN through the facility, the alarm began to sound. Eventually, they came upon a hallway that had windows along one side of it. Marc stopped running when he looked out through the windows. A large, underground hangar, where hundreds of the ships, similar to the ones they encountered, were docked. Several varieties were visible to them, larger ships and smaller ships. Fleets of them were prepared. Everyone stopped running when they noticed Marc was looking through the windows.

"How far is the broadcast center?" Marc asked.

"Right behind this door is a lift that will take us directly to the room and an exit." Carla said.

Marc continued to look down at the large chamber. Guards were rushing boxes into the larger ships. It seemed they were evacuating. But through the movement and crowds of soldiers, Marc could see one general; Apollo.

"You guys go ahead of me." Marc said. "I'll meet you guys up at the surface. I need to handle some business."

"I'm staying with you." John said. "You know I always have your back, Marc. No matter what."

"No!" Marc said. "I need you to destroy the broadcast center for me. Can you do that for me?" Marc asked, as he looked John in the eyes.

"Yeah, I got it." John reluctantly said. John and the others ran to the other side of the hallway and ran through the doorway. John nodded to Marc as the automatic doors closed. Marc then turned and smashed through a window. It was several hundred feet from the window to the floor of the hangar. But Marc only fell several dozen feet before he shot forward in flight.

"Incoming!" A guard yelled when he heard the window shatter. This caused Apollo to turn and see Marc shooting directly toward him.

"C and R protocol!" Apollo barked out. "This one is mine alone." He said with a laugh.

The guards dropped what they were doing and began rushing into the ships. Marc slammed into Apollo, forcing him to smash into he floor. Apollo then placed a palm against Marc's chest, and then a blast of wind threw Marc back into the air. Apollo began flying toward Marc. Marc began throwing fireballs at Apollo from the air. Apollo shifted sided to side to avoid the blasts. Apollo then slammed into Marc, forcing him to smash against the wall. Doors began to open as more guards poured into the room. The guards were not there to fight, they were evacuating.

* * *

As the lift reached the top level, the sentinels ran out. The building looked like a storage facility from the outside. In fact, it looked like the warehouse they found in Borrow. The only difference is that this warehouse was full of expensive equipment that was still completely operational. John ran to a large computer that had the image of a satellite on the monitor. John began to randomly press buttons.

"Do you know what you're doing?" Ignacia asked as she watched John chaotically work the controls.

"I'm making my hours of video games worth while." John said as he smashed his palm against all the keys. When he did this, a warning flashed across the screen. The warning read 'Malfunction: Planet Fall!'. "Ok, we can go." John said. "My job is done here."

When he and Ignacia reached the outside, the ground was rumbling. All the other sentinels were stopped in their tracks.

"What's going on?" John asked. "I don't think we should just be standing around like this." He added nervously.

Then the ground in front of them began to split open. The entire land in front of them was the entrance to the underground hangar. The opening stretched to half a mile wide. Ships began to shoot out of the opening.

* * *

Marc threw a large sonic blast at Apollo; Apollo's new armor was protecting well against electrical and thermal attacks, but sonic and rock attacks were still doing damage. Marc noticed the attacks were not doing enough damage to end the fight quickly; he knew the other generals would be coming soon.

Marc was slammed against the ground by a force of wind that could only be described as a typhoon. Marc looked around as he tried to force his body to stand against the wind. He saw several containers that were labeled 'Reserve Fuel'. He then saw a fueling station by the containers; he believed this was the answer to his problem.

[John.] Marc said as he began to form a firewall to counter the winds. [John, where the hell are you?]

[You need help?] John asked; something seemed odd about his 'voice'.

[No, but I need you to get as far away from here as possible.] Marc said. [I'm ganna replay the gas station fight.]

[I would,] John said. [But we have our hands full with some very annoying metal-heads.]

[Which ones?] Marc asked as he threw a sonic blast with one hand while holding the firewall with the other.

* * *

John threw a bolt of lighting from his hands and into the chest of a mecha-soldier. Ignacia was lobbing fireballs at several other soldiers as she hovered just inches from the ground like a fiery phantom.

The Mecha-soldiers looked a lot like the generals, in a sense that they were completely covered in cybernetic armor. They all had their right hands turned into some sort of cannon that fired a variety of munitions: shotgun sprays, single round shot, and large caliber bullets.

[They're a bunch of no-names.] John said. [But they are dropping like flies. Just give us like five minutes.]

A larger ship had landed by the station and released several dozen mecha-soldiers. John was striking as many as he could with lighting. Ignacia was torching each one she could hit with a fiery grenade. Greg was smashing each one that got too close to him with his marble-strong arms. Carla and Blanca were shooting beams of light that blasted through several soldiers at a time. Isaac was firing sonic booms that shattered any mecha-soldier that was caught in its range. Alex was scooping up snow and forcing it into sharp shards of ice and flinging them into soldiers. Tobias was forcing wind-spikes to throw soldiers hundreds of feet away. And Amber was forcing seeds from her hands and throwing them to the ground; vines sprouted out of the seeds and wrapped around the soldiers, the soldiers were then being smashed together by the monstrous vines.

* * *

[Fine.] Marc said as he began flying toward Apollo at neck-breaking speed. [But this five minutes is only ganna last you like two minutes!] Marc added.

Apollo flew at Marc at the same speed. Both brawlers smashed into each other; each one landed a fist on the other. Marc's sonic-charged fist slammed into Apollo's face; Apollo's wind-boosted fist collided with Marc's body. Marc was thrown back against a wall and Apollo was thrown back and smashed into the ground on his back.

Marc Began running toward Apollo, who looked to be having trouble getting up. As Marc was just about to drop a large, stone fist, Apollo aimed both palms at him. Marc was tossed back by a powerful blast of wind. He landed by the fueling station. Apollo shot out at Marc with both fists out in front.

Marc let out a powerful blast of electricity that caused the fuel tanks to explode. Apollo was now trying to stop, but he was flying to fast to stop in time; he flew into the blue flame that erupted from the tanks. The explosion ignited the fueling station and after a few moments, the entire fuel reserve exploded. The explosion launched a massive fireball that blacked the sky. The force of the explosion coursed through the entire compound; it began to collapse. Marc shot out of the flames and into the sky. He was searching the ground for his friends but the ground had begun to cave into the compound for miles.

[Where is everyone?] Marc asked franticly. He was worried they didn't make it far enough away in time.

[Look up, zángano!] John said. Marc immediately looked up and saw a large ship hovering thousands of feet in the air. The sentinels had taken the one that the mecha-soldiers had arrived in.

[How are you guys flying that?] Marc asked as he began to fly upward toward the ship.

[I'm flying it.] Isaac said. [The controls are the same on each ship. I just need someone to tell me where we are going.] He explained. [Landing is ganna be a pain in the ass though.] He joked.

Marc laughed, as he got closer to the ship. But his movement was stalled as a silver blur shot right past him; it was Apollo. Apollo smashed into one of the ships engines. The ship began to spiral out of control and fall.

"No!" Marc cried out as he fired a green orb of light at Apollo. The pulsating orb exploded as it hit Apollo across the chest; his armor nearly shattering by the force of the attack as he dropped hundreds of feet to the ground.

Marc began flying straight down to catch up with the falling ship. He was getting closer and closer to the ship, but the ship was getting closer and closer to crashing into the ground. *I need to stop it! I can't lose them!* Marc thought to himself as he was just a few feet from the ship's bottom. . . . . .

CHAPTER 35:

PRELUDE TO A DESTROYER

APOLLO STOOD AT ATTENTION in front of the man in the suit; who was sitting at his desk. A nameplate on his desk read 'Abraham I. Truman'. Apollo was still in his damaged armor. He had his facemask off, revealing the true face of Jake Evens.

"It's ok." Abraham said. "I, once again, anticipated your failure, Apollo. Perhaps I will leave Hates in charge of an evacuation, instead of you."

"Sir, I apologize for letting him get away. . ." Apollo began to say, but was interrupted by Abraham.

"You think I am disappointed in you letting him

escape?" Abraham asked with a sarcastic smile. "You let him destroy a multibillion dollar facility!" he barked at Apollo. "Get out of my site." He added.

Apollo began to walk out of Abraham's office, but stopped just at the door.

"Sir," Apollo said. "What is the plan now?" he asked, repeating Athena's unanswered question.

"You are on a need to know basis." Abraham said as he reached for a file in his desk. "And right now, you don't need to know."

"Sir, with all due respect," Apollo said as he walked back over to the desk. "I am your High General and I need to know. . ." he was once again interrupted by Abraham.

"You are one of my High Generals." Abraham said. Apollo paused fore a moment.

"I'm sorry but what?" Apollo asked.

"You are one of three High Generals." Abraham said as he gave the file to Apollo. The file contained every generals score on their performance test. "The top three are High Generals." Abraham said.

The paper read:

Echo: 19/100
Athena: 20/100
Poseidon: 24/100
Zeus: 29/ 100
Aries: 36/100
Coronus: 42/100
Hercules: 69/100
Apollo: 89/100
Hates: 94/100
Morning Star: 100/100

"Sir, who is Morning Star?" Apollo asked as he read the paper. He was outraged to know that he was below two more people; one of which did not have a fully functional brain.

"He is my masterpiece." Abraham said. "I found someone who was a match to be the multi-elemental anomaly. So I had no need for this Marcus Salazar's blood sample, I just needed to fuse his blood with the gene in my son's blood. Like I did with Poseidon and Athena." Abraham explained.

"When can I expect to meet Morning Star?" Apollo asked. He was still staring at the score Morning Star received on his performance test.

"You will meet him when you need to meet him." Abraham said. "Right now, I want you to go to the lab so we can apply your new armor."

"New armor, Sir?" Apollo asked. He thought he was already wearing his new armor. "What do you mean, Sir?"

"I have decided that I want my High Generals wearing more appealing armor." Abraham said. "And inconveniently enough, you are one of my High Generals." He added.

"Very well, Sir." Apollo said as he walked out.

CHAPTER 36:

ALONE

MARC SAT ALONE AT a bar in Anchorage, Alaska. There were other people at the bar, which seemed to be doing good on this particular day, but no one that Marc knew. He was wearing his sunglasses so no one would notice that one eye was glowing dark green. He had a half full mug in one hand; the other arm was just resting on the bar.

[So I think we won.] Marc said to the First.

[You didn't.] The First replied. [If you had won, you wouldn't be talking to me right now.]

[Well I don't know what else to do.] Marc said. [I blew up the lab, I got all the elements, and I'm sure I killed one of the major bad guys.] Marc said

[Being sure isn't knowing.] The First argued. [I know this is a lot to ask, but you can't abandon this campaign.]

[Campaign?] Marc asked. [This isn't a war.]

[Yes it is, Marc! It's your war, and you need to keep doing what is necessary!] The First said. [Marc, we can't let Abraham continue with his plan. You have to stop him.]

[You want me to go after him?] Marc asked. [After what happened to my friends, you want me to chase after that?] Marc was getting annoyed.

[I had to sacrifice a lot too, you know?] The First said. [I had all the same responsibilities you do. What makes you any different?] He asked.

[What did you ever sacrifice?] Marc asked out of doubt. He took a drink from his mug.

[I sacrificed my life!] The First shouted. [Listen you ungrateful little brat! You were blessed with these abilities to protect everything you care about. Like your mother.]

[What do you mean?] Marc asked.

[Nothing.] The First said. [I meant you could protect people like your mother.] The First hesitated. Marc noticed this.

[No!] Marc said. [What do you know about my mother?] He asked. [Why did you bring her up?]

[How much do you know about your mom?] The First asked. [How much do you really know about her?]

[What are you trying to say?] Marc asked. [Was my mom a sentinel?] He continued.

[You really like that Amber girl, don't you?] The First asked. [You think she's really pretty, don't you?]

[Yeah, but what does that have to do with my mother?] Marc asked confused.

[Sometimes, guys tend to pick a girl just like their mother.] The First joked.

[My mom fought for you?] Marc asked in awe. The First did not answer; he had severed the connection.

Marc finished his drink and left a tip on the bar as he stood up. He proceeded to walk out of the bar and down the street. He was the only one not wearing a jacket. After a few short seconds, Marc heard someone calling his name from behind him. He turned to see who it was.

"Hey Marc, where are you going?" John asked as he reached Marc. Everyone is at the restaurant down the street. Come on, I saved you a seat."

"John, we have to talk." Marc said sternly.

"What's wrong?" John asked as his face went from cheerful serious. "What happened?"

"It's not over." Marc said. "It turns out this thing is bigger than we thought." He added.

"Well you know I always have your back, Marc." John said as he lightly slapped Marc's shoulder.

"That's it, John." Marc said. "I don't think I want you guys to risk your lives." John thought for a moment after hearing Marc's statement.

"Listen, Marc," John started. "I know you're the leader and what not, but you can't tell me what to do." He joked. "Now let's get some grub." He added.

"Fine." Marc said. "But we're talking about this later."

"What ever." John replied. The two began walking down the street together.

Chapter 37:

Nightmares to Come

That night, Marc and the others had decided to spend the night in a hotel, to relax mainly. But Marc did it to sleep. He was tired for some reason. Then he heard an echo in his head. The echo was a voice that he had never heard before.

"Chimera." The voice said.

Marc lay down in his bed and began to sleep. He felt his body shutting down. The voice was putting him to sleep as it continued to speak.

"I am the Essence." The voice said. "I have foreseen what your acts will bring to this world. Allow me to show you what will come to pass."

Marc opened his eyes. He was standing in the middle of a large city square. The buildings were battle scarred and breaking apart. It looked like several bombs had gone off everywhere. The streets around the empty square were packed with screaming people. They seemed to be crying and pleading to Marc for something. He could not hear their cries. They sounded distant and muffled.

Marc looked around in confusion. He saw Ignacia burning; she was screaming and grabbing at her hair in frustration. He saw Greg chained to the floor; tired and weak. He only saw one of the twins; she was weeping blood. He saw Tobias laying flat on his back; not moving. Alex was dragging himself along the ground, gasping for breath. But John, Amber, and Isaac were nowhere in site.

In the blink of an eye, everyone was gone. Marc looked around until he saw a man standing on the opposite side of the city square. The man was wearing a black cloak. Marc could not see his face. He could hear the man laughing.

"Who are you?" Marc shouted. The man continued to laugh. Marc readied a fireball in his right hand. "You better tell me who you are!" he warned.

"I am the Morning Star." The man said in a demonic voice. "And I will end your existence!" The man shouted as he shot out toward Marc like a bullet. Morning Star was flying just inches from the ground. A wall of dust was rising behind him as he approached Marc.

As Marc threw his fireball at Morning Star, he awoke. The sun was out. He was in his hotel room. Marc then scrambled to his feet. He looked at the clock beside the bed; it was dawn.

"What the hell was that?" John asked from the corner of the room. Marc had not seen him sitting in the chair.

"What the hell was what?' Marc asked. Marc was trying to hide his fear. This was impossible since he was sweating a cascade and his heart was beating like a drum line.

"You were saying some freaky stuff in your sleep." John replied as he stood up.

"Have you been watching me all night?" Marc asked as he walked toward the bathroom.

"Just when you started screaming." John said worried. Marc said nothing from the bathroom.

"What was I screaming?" Marc said as he walked out of the bathroom.

"You said Morning Star like ten times." John said. He looked even more worried. "That's the Devil, Marc." John informed.

"It was just a nightmare." Marc said, trying to calm John down. "That's all it was, ok?" John was not the only one he was trying to convince.

"Ok." John said. "Come on, let's get some breakfast." He said as his mood instantly changed.

"Where is everyone?" Marc asked as they left the room.

"Everyone is already eating breakfast." John said. "So where are we headed from here?" he asked.

Marc thought for a moment. It's been months since they've been home, but they could never return; Apollo knew their identities. So where could they go from here, he thought.

"Let's go down to Amber's place to check in on the family." Marc said. "Then maybe we should head out to New York City." He added.

"New York?" John repeated as he followed Marc down the hallway. He was fiddling with the cross on his necklace. "Well, I guess it wouldn't hurt."

To Be Continued in Elements Of War
Volume 2: Dawn